D1549560

When Your Associates R More Dangerous Than U
Copyright © 2006

LCCN:2007906991
ISBN:978-0-9797836-0-9
Cover Design/Graphics:Melissa Underwood, Say No
More Graphics
Photography:Damon Riddick, Skolar Media &
Entertainment, www.skolargrafix.com

FOR INFORMATION CONTACT:
Grown Man Publishing, LLC

Grown Man Publishing, LLC
P.O. Box 514
Jeffersonville, IN 47130
canonharper@icloud.com

This Book Is Dedicated To My
Grandparents
Houston and Jenny High
You two are my Heros!

My Corner

My Mother, you always fault yourself for our self destructive ways. Well its time for you to rejoice in one of my greatest accomplishments. If you hadn't introduced us to the life, that we love, I wouldn't be able to give indebt accounts of "The Game," in my writing.

Gina, you've given me three beautiful children, always supported me and endured a helluva struggle, while I beefed with the Feds and the State. Thanks for being so strong. I love you.

Thell, what can I say. You're my brother, my rappi—my best friend. We're million dollar dudes, and this is only the first venture to start us on the new road that we're traveling.

Cari, my baby sister. Keep doing what choo do. Its so nice to have a sibling with such focus and talent. I may be the first one to put our family out there, but you'll be the most successful—NO DOUBT!

My life lines: CaNon, Tea, and Te'Sean. You three are the motivation behind my change in lifestyle. If not for you I'd probably be Tay, in oppose to creating him. Daddy Loves You!

Much Love

My ole man Carthell, my late grandparents James and
Melissa Harper, my aunts LaDonna the Diva (R.I.P),
Cynthia, and Mary, my uncle Bub, Van, Meek, Tamika,
Rodney, Brian, Sonya, Mark, Anthony, Dae-Dae, Kim,
LaKeisa, Linda, Antoine, Chris, Simone, Earlette, Gia,
Auntie Deb, Joy, Bridget, Elise, Beverly, Burt, Derek,
Margie, Gwen, Aunt Laura, Mr. Hubbard(R.I.P), Mel,
Pat, Erica, Krystal, Mike—you jumped on board to get this
jumping. Good looking out; Granny, Trelle, Philicia, Boss,
Lettie, Lonnie, Lana, Samatra, Ms. Sanders—you are the
best Executive Assistant a man could have, Billy, Eric,
Neicy, Marcel, Jackie, Sharice, Ciara, Sharell, Ray, Mr.
Stephen, Big Brian, Caprice and Brittany.

Soldier Love

Skinny ScuRelli (R.I.P) Pony Down, Lea—luck and good
karma got me a sidekick like you, Tony, Zo, Malik,
Dre- Bey, Dre, Jay, M.B., Head—good looking out on the
typewriter and the late night snacks, Boob(R.I.P), Pots,
Virg, Batty, Blah, Eric(R.I.P), Smokey, Lee, Carlos, A.D.,
Lil E (R.I.P), Stoney, Young Boy Down, Money Mark,
Doo-Doo, Burt, T.J., Cool Cat, Indoe, Quick Curt, 6 Mile
Curt, Flea, Tone Buckner, The Bear, Butter, A.J., Sterling,
Bee—the rich Texan, Snoop, Jo-Jo, Black, Scoob, Dice,
Junior, Kyle, Dave, Ed, Frank Nitty, Black, Kendron-you
a true playa fa real, Rico—thanks for all the advice you've
given me, young Flynn, Thad. And all those that I forgot,
you know the saying.

Special Thanks

Angelena Sanders, you got this project where it is! If not for you I'd probably still have this project in its infant stages. Thanks Beautiful!

Anthony Thornton, you came thru for your lil cousin like the trooper you are. Good looking out homie! Now let's push it to the limit!

Ashawn Cole, so many females sold me out, but not you. I shoulda known that I needed a FRIEND to help me complete my goal! And you the SEXIEST anyway!

Cecil Clark, black boy you always come thru fa me. What's understood need not be spoken. However, I must say thank you!

Last, but not underappreciated, Melissa Underwood from Say No More Graphics. You did a wonderful job on the logos, and the cover is a KNOCKOUT. Yall keep doing ya thang! www.snmgraphics.com

"EYE'S OF A GHETTO CHILD"

Eye's wide open wit' limited sight
Can see da plights that fa a kid ain't right
Da home houses a parent that provides no guidance
Da streets and da hood is surrounded wit' violence
Grown up choices being made
By the time ya in 4th grade
By da 6th or 7th ya toting a weapon
And a few of ya mans been slayed
Lifes so ugly that ya wanna vomit
But that's fa kids wit weak stomach'
Ya too young ta know ya callin'
But old enough ta know loot calms it
Hate wearing shoes wit no name
Or ones ya embarrassed ta say
Which is crazy in da Ghetto we all livin' da same way
Shame drives ya down a road lead by a man wit' horns and a pitch fork
At the ends a door and once ya walk thru livin' lifes' a total joy
Of course there's a price
Da ultimate cha life
But it you'll sacrifice
Ta escape da mice da roach being and dreadin' night cause there's no lights
That's the life of my peers dat white folks fear and cringe at cause its foul
That's the life of my peers that I luv ta death cause I too am a Ghetto Child

I hopped in da car wit' shame in 'bout 8th grade so I guess I was 'bout 12
Sick of bread and syrup clothes from K-mart and that house on a street called hell
My grades ain't matter I could read spell and count so I knew which route I'd take

It was far from strait more like a figure 8 and a helluva game ta play
Didn't like da police
Ain't wanna help da sickly
Or defend guys like me
Wanted ta cop cook cut weigh dope fa money that's tax free
Move rocks on da block around the clock cranking till da corners hot
Then its in a house called a spot doe locked moving it through a slot
Sleep is unheard of ya learn ta cat nap and that'll be at the end of da month
But if ya yay is butter da boulders blocked like kiss that spot gon' rock
Afta a month non-stop and ya avoided da cops ya finally come on out
Carrying da stench of a week old corpse but cha pockets can't hold ya knots
Da content hit da mall and blow doh on clothes and shoes
Whereas da ambitious call da big man and wait fa him ta come thru
I feel da content but admire da ambitious cause I too want more than gear
But rather be content than stay stuck in da ghetto doin' nothin' and my eye's
shedin tears

When no longer pumpin' rocks and up ta movin' weight
You graduate to da next level and there's even more at stake
Now seen as a lick ta those dat ain't got shit
Da target ta rival crews whose business ya interfere wit'
Jealousy and envy dude you need ta be privy too
And da rats dat got knocked and plan ta get they break off you
Not ta mention da police
Low lifes workin' da streets and precincts
Or what's on da mind of a chick acting giddy afta a drink
Da minds always second guessin'
Years in da streets taught dat lesson
Is it real does she really dig me?
Or is she da bait so her mans can hit me
And when a cat wants ta re-up
Is it real or a set-up

And if so is it fa da yay
Or part of his deal wit' da D.A.
Gotta ask these questions ta protect self
And effectively play da hand ya dealt
Money's made life much betta and mo' hectic
Receding hair line and grays in da beard reflect it
But thru it all I've matured and no longer wild
And smile
Still dat Ghetto Child

CaNon

When Your Associates R More Dangerous Than U

Part 1

A Livin' Hell Can Be Made Convenient

... They send me to a level 3 yard that's where I stay.
Late night I hear toothbrushes scrapping on the floor.
Niggas getting they shanks just in case the war pops off...

Snoop Dogg

1

Chapter One

"Now what's 'bout to happen?" I asked.

"Shid, once one of the C.O.'s see dude they're gonna blow emergency count. Then we'll be locked down for a day or two.

"Get a couple of books and mags when you get back to da unit."

I had just gotten off the bus and hit the compound. As I was walking to the unit they assigned me to, I saw my man Sig from my neighborhood. Sig had been down since '92.

"What up doe my nigga! Cats from da way told me you got knocked."

"Yeah. These bitches broke me off a eight piece. What I gotta do off that?"

"Dontae, ain't no need in talking 'bout out-dates and good time, fish ass nigga."

"Damn! Da joint done made you a first name calling muthaphucka," I said, laughing.

"Naw. But I'm serious Tay. You gotta learn ta do your bit or it will do you, strait up."

With a smile on my face I looked at Sig and said, "Alright Nelson. Well, since I can't inquire about my out-date, can I inquire about how I can get some buds in my system?"

"Ain't no doubt. What unit you in?"

"They told me ta go to C unit."

"Ooh Shit! That's Ms. Massey's unit. Let's go drop your bed roll off. You gon' love looking at her every day."

Once we left my unit and headed up to the rec yard, it started to sink in. 'Damn,' I thought to myself, 'I'm actually in da joint.' It didn't look anything like I had envisioned it. It actually looked like a college campus. The unit really tripped me out. The cells almost looked like dorm rooms, and they had pool and ping pong tables in them.

"Tasha was phucked up when you got sentenced whatn't she?"

"Ain't no doubt. When the judge said, 'I sentence you to 96 months', she broke down cryin'. The numbers ninety six, alone, probably phucked 'er up."

"Hell yeah! I already know dog. Them girls feel lost when we're taken away. BUT, they get over it, real fast."

"Dog, Tasha was crying so hard that I thought it was gonna be harmful to the baby."

With a shocked look, and a grin on his face, Sig looked at me and asked, "What baby?"

"Oh, you ain't know?"

"Naw!"

"Man, she's three months pregnant. While I was out on bond fighting my case, we spent all of our time together, 'cause I knew I was gon get hit. So I was O.D.ing in 'er so she'd have a reminder of myself."

Sig, apparently misunderstood my reason for wanting Tash to have my seed, 'cause he started laughing and said, "You a silly dude. Babies don't stop them girls from doing what they wanna do."

"That whan't my reason for…Damn, they phuckin' dude up!"

"Oh yeah. The D.C niggas be off da hook. They wild like Detroit niggas. It's just that we more so be on that paper chase."

"It looks like they 'bout to kill dude. Is it like this every day?"

"Naw. A lot of the time it's pretty laid back, but when it goes down, it goes down. C'mon, let's get up outta here."

We hit the track and started kicking it. Sig said that he should see somebody that had some trees. We were completing our first lap when about six cats walked out of the gym looking at us, with their mugs ripped. I got a 'And Whut?' look on my face, figuring that it's about to be on with these cats. I recognized two of them from the altercation in the gym, then Sig started giving dap and introducing me to them. I should have known he'd be plugged in with the fools, 'cause he's always in the mix of the shit that's happening.

"What up doe? Where da trees at Ito?" Sig asked the short stocky dude.

"You know I got 'em. Just got 'em as a matter of fact. That country ass nigga in the gym thought he was gon be on 'round this bitch. Know we ain't havin' that."

"Well, what's happening? Me and my mans wanna get right. Show love to a made man."

"Stamps or send in? Either or, or both. You know I like to fill my lungs and got the doh with flags and presidents on it. I'm a muthaphuckin' patriot!"

I saw that Sig hadn't changed. He was still silly, liked to get high, and didn't like to even think people were questioning his money.

"Dig, give me 250 in stamps and send me 250 for 40 caps. I'll give 'em to you tomorrow, 'cause I gotta sack that shit up, but I'll throw you something to smoke tonight, just on the strength, yunno."

"Bet. My man. You want me to shoot it to da same hook up you gave me before?"

"Yeah. Let me go in da bathroom and snatch sumin' out fa you. I'll be right back."

While we were waiting, they announced over the loud speaker, "The recreation yard is closed. One way move back to the housing units." I later learned that you go to and from when they had a 10 minute move, or an open move.

When Ito came back, Sig told him, "My man Tay is in your unit. Give 'im some lockdown material fa me."

"Aiight, that ain't shit.
"Shid, what room did they put choo in? I ain't got a bunky. You might be in my room."

"I think it was 2137", I said as I tried to remember.

"Was it some bad ass females in bikinis on da board?"

"Yeah".

"That's Yahmo's room. He's from Cali. That's why all them pictures are taken on beaches."

"Is he aiight?"

"Yeah, he's laid back, keeps to his self, and he smokes, so yall should get along."

When Sig got the trees from Ito, he told him "good looking. I'm out, and that'll be on da way as soon as I can get on da phone." He gave me a play and said "I'll holla at choo when they let us out to play again."

Me and Ito kicked it as we walked back to the unit. Once we got back to the unit he gave me some Black and Mild cigars and a few XXL magazines. When I walked in my room there were some papers on my bunk. As I picked them up to see what they were, my bunky walked in and the officer locked the door behind him.

"These yours?" I asked, holding the papers out toward him.

"Yeah. That's my PSI and trial transcript. Feel free to read that so you'll know I ain't no rat. I don't phuck wit' rats, so if you're hot, as soon as you can, you need to move up outta here."

Understandingly nodding my head, I said, "My name is Tay. I'm from Detroit, I got my PSI, some trees, and I'll get my transcripts sent as soon as I call my lawyer. Now. Can I make up my bunk?"

Extending his hand, he said, "They call me Yahmo. If the stress is good, proceed to make up your bunk so we can get high."

Chapter Two

"This bitch ain't gon leave the house until she hears from Dontae," Trina said, looking at Yolanda. They had come over to try to get Tasha out the house.

Tasha was tired of listening to Trina act like she was mad about her wanting to her from her man. "Bitch, are you happy that he hasn't called or mad that I love my man and wanna hear from him?"

Yolanda knew that Tasha was stressing with Dontae being locked up. She also knew that she better try an calm her down before it escalated to a physical altercation. "Look Tasha, Trina just doesn't like seeing you so depressed. We love you and wanna help you get through this ordeal. But don't hate us because we don't want you to put your life on hold."

"She's right" Trina said. "I don't mean to sound insensitive, but Dontae's choices landed him in jail. You shouldn't confine yourself to a room for nothin'." The look on Tasha's face told Trina that she had misunderstood her. "An I'm not saying Tay ain't nothing, I mean..."

Before she could finish her sentence Tasha cut her off. "Just phuck it! I don't expect you to understand me and Dontae's bond. Or anything about loyalty. Tone wasn't gone six months before you had a nigga up in the house; that he bought for you!"

Yolanda had heard enough. "Yall bitches trippin'! We getting ready to go so you can get some rest and chill out", she said as she grabbed her purse and gave Tasha a hug. Trina hugged Tasha too, but chose to keep her mouth shut.

Every since Dontae had gone to prison Tasha hadn't wanted to do but sit in the house and wait for his calls. She couldn't believe he hadn't called in two days. It's bad enough that she hadn't been able to see him since he had been moved from the county. "I'm 'bout to go crazy in this house." Damn, look at me, I'm starting to talk to myself, out loud, she thought. Figuring that she should take Trina and Landa's advice, she reached for the phone.

"Hello."

"Hey Ma" she said, relieved that her mother was home.

"Hi Baby. I was gonna call you as soon as I finished doing laundry. How are you holding up?"

That was a question that Tasha wasn't sure of. Being alone and pregnant definitely wasn't her idea of doing well, but she wouldn't let her mother know that she was falling apart. "I've had better days, but I'm cool. I was calling to see if you wanted to go shopping, then to dinner?"

"Of course, I'd love to spend the day with my beautiful daughter. Plus, your Daddy is in the doghouse, so as you youngsters say, I'm a pat his wallet."

Her mother was always messing up the sayings. Laughing, she said, "Ma, its hit his pockets. And you leave my daddy alone. Where is he anyway?"

"The Pistons are playing, so you know he's in the basement in front of the TV smoking one of them funny cigarettes. You wanna talk to 'im?"

"Naw. I'll see him when I get there. See ya in a minute."

"Okay. Bye Baby."

During the ride to her parents house Tasha thought about Dontae and how perfect her life had seemed three months ago. Even with the case and the probability of him doing time, she never imagined feeling like this. A little over 90 days ago, April 6, 1996, she had been the happiest woman in the world. She had turned 21 and received the best news of her young life. That whole day was full of surprises.

******

"Hello," she said, answering the phone.

"May I speak to Ratasha Foster?"

"Speaking."

"This is Doctor Lane's office. The doctor would like to talk with you. Please hold."

The lady didn't sound like the news was bad, but she wouldn't know, Tasha thought nervously. She had been on edge every since yesterday after taking that test.

"Ms. Foster?"

"Yes. How are you Dr. Lane?"

"I'm fine. I'm calling to tell you that we have the results of your fertility test. Would you like to come in?"

"No. I'd rather you just tell me now." Her heart was beating at a rapid pace. The fact that he asked if she wanted to meet face to face gave her an uneasy feeling."

"Well, not only are there no problems, but you're going to be a mom."

Tasha started grinning from ear to ear. "Are you serious?" she exclaimed.

"Very much so. Probably a few weeks, so I want you to make an appointment to come in, ASAP. Okay?"

"All right. Thank you, Dr. Lane."

"You're very welcome, and, congratulations."

She walked into the living room and stood in front of Dontae beaming. He looked up at her from the couch and said, "Baby what choo so happy about? Did we hit da lotto?"

"No." she answered, making a silly face at him, "just take a guess, Daddy."

Reflecting over his sexual prowess from the night before, he smiled and said, "I knew four was gon send you over the top, but don't get spoiled. Two or three is what you should expect. I'll give you four when you're a good girl. Even though four takes all my energy."

"Baby, I'm pregnant," she said and playfully raised my hand like I was about to hit him.

With wide open eyes and a half smile on his face, he looked up at her and asked "for real?" Tasha just stood there nodding her head, "yes." Dontae stood up with his arms open to receive her and said, "C'mere and give Daddy a kiss".

Looking up at him with her arms around his neck, she said "Well Baby, we got what we wanted." He kissed her, grabbed her hand, and then told her, "close your eyes". Leading her to the front door, he opened it and they stepped out onto the porch.

"Happy birthday Tash."

When she opened her eyes, sitting in the driveway, behind his white Cadillac DeVille/DTS was a silver Mercedes SL55 AMG with berry interior, wrapped with a huge red ribbon. She turned around, with tears in her eyes, "Thank you Baby," as he was handing her keys to her new car.

*****

By the time Tasha pulled up in front of her parents house she wanted to turn around and go back home, but that would only leave her all alone to sulk even more, so she grabbed some tissue out of her purse, dried her eyes, and then went in the house.

Chapter Three

After being cooped up in that cell for two days, I was anxious to get up outta that unit. As soon as they opened the yard I shot down to Sig's unit. "Aye, get Sig up outta there fa me," I told this cat walking into A unit.

Sig was 5'10" and weighed about 210 pounds. He had a scar on the left side of his face from a botched robbery that gave his physical appearance a hardened look. When he came out of the unit with a sweatshirt, shower shoes and a doo-rag on, he looked just like a convict. "Young Tay, whut up doe! A couple of day's on lock down got choo up and out."

"Ain't no doubt. I had enough rest. Let's shoot up top, put a few in us and kick it."

With a smirk on his face, Sig looked at me like I was crazy and said, "You know I blew that lil shit I had. I gotta holla at Ito."

"He just gave it to me when I was leaving out the unit."

"Bet. Let me go grab my Blacks. I'll be right back."

While I waited on Sig, I wondered where Tash was. I'd tried to call her twice that morning but didn't get an answer. Once they called the eleven o'clock 10 minute move, I decided to go holla at Sig and get out of the unit for an hour or two.

"So, how did you get knocked?" Sig asked me, as we headed up to the rec yard.

Knowing that this subject wasn't going to be a five minute conversation, I told him, "We'll kick it when we get up top. You gonna trip too. I was slipping and got knocked on some phuck shit."

"Nigga, I done been in this Federal system fa four years now. Don't shit surprise me no more. Unless you tell me you couldn't hold your water," Sig said, with a smirk on his face.

"I put twelve in that box! And kept what I know to myself. I'm playing this game like its 'spose to be played. Enjoyed the Benjamin's and going to endure the bit."

Once we passed through the medal detectors, Sig dipped into the gym to go into the bathroom. I continued strait and walked through the second set of double doors outside to the rec yard. "I guess this is an everyday thing," I thought to myself as I glance around the yard. Dudes lifting weights on the pile to the left. Cats sitting in the bleachers by the softball field kickin' it. And, on the other side of the yard, various groups standing around talking, while others were on the court 'Eight years of this repetitious ass shit,' I was thinking when I heard my name. Looking toward the weight pit, I saw my bunky walking toward me. "Young Yahmo I see you out here getting your best physical fitness on."

"You know it. I ain't got but a few more year's" Yahmo said as he gave me some dap. "What's up wit' choo?"

As I turned to see if Sig was coming, I said "Waiting on Sig so we can get high. You smoking?"

"Naw. Yall go 'head."

"Aiight, my man, I'll holla at choo later," I told him as I went to meet Sig on the bleachers by the softball field.

*****

I looked around the yard then looked at Sig and said, "I'm high as hell!"

Sig busted out laughing. "Damn Tay, we still got anotha blunt. Don't pass out."

My eyes were bloodshot red and halfway closed when I looked at Sig and said, "Nigga, I ain't smoking anotha nothin'. I'm almost at the stage where I'm ready to promise God that I won't get high no'mo if he lets me make it."

Laughing so hard that he had tears in his eyes, Sig grabbed my hand to pull me up and said, "Let's hit the track. We got 'bout two hours before count."

"So, how'd you get knocked? One minute I'm hearing that you're out there getting money, then next thing I know I'm hearing you done been indicted."

Shaking my head, I looked at Sig and began to tell him how this nightmare, that I'm now living, started. "Dog, when you caught your case, I got real focused. Remember, I would get eighteen or a whole thang from you, but wasn't strivin' ta get rich?"

Sig knew exactly what I was talking 'bout. He was a few years older than me, and whenever I would cop from him, he'd say, 'I hope you're stacking your change. This game don't last forever.' Looking me over, he'd say, 'Every time I see you, between your jewels and gear, you look like you blowin' all your profits and there's just enough for re-upin'.'

And he'd be damn near right. But once I heard that when he got knocked, he was holdin' 'bout $300,000.00, cash in the car, I was like, **'DAMN'**. Then, what really phucked me up was that it was paper he had after he'd left the after hour spot.

"You had a few hundred stacks on you when you caught this case, didn't choo?" I had to ask, just to see how accurate the word on the street was.

Wit' a crooked grin on his face, Sig said, "They popped me wit' two and some change. I told 'em ta keep it and let me go. Instead, they took me in and said I had a hundred and twenty-five thousand, but that's a whole notha story. Go 'head."

"Yeah. So, when I heard that, I was like DAMN! You was playing wit' more than I had stacked. At that point it was time for me to take thangs more serious."

The weed had Sig paying close attention. "Who did you start phuckin' wit' when I got locked up?' He asked, as he freaked his Black and Mild.

"Did you know Travis? He's off da east side."

Looking like he was trying to put a face wit' the name, he finally shook his head, and said, "Naw."

"Well, anyway, I was wit' dude for 'bout a year, but I had to start shopping elsewhere."

"Why? What happened?"

I took a hit off the Black and said, "He couldn't give me no love. I'm tryin' ta grab between five and seven, and he wanna charge me nineteen a piece. I was paying nineteen five for one or two."

Sig looked at me grinning and said, "You sure missed me, didn't choo?"

"You already know I did. But, I found a nice plug and shit picked up. After you left and I put shit in perspective, hustling and Tasha was all that I was focused on. Then I got a major line at the end of '93 and was able to take shit to a whole notha level. In '95 I figured I'd take Tasha to Paris for her 20th birthday."

"Damn! You was like phuck a cruise and the Bahamas; you was gon do it big, huh?" Sig asked, giving me a play.

"Ain't no doubt. Up until February of '95 I had been all work and no play. So I was gon enjoy that bread. But the same day that I was going to see the travel agent, my lawyer called and told me to come see 'im."

Sig looked at me and said, "You knew somethin' was wrong then, didn't choo?"

"Hell yeah. Man, I went ta see this lame, and he told me the Fed's was gon indict me on da 4th of April."

"Damn, that just phucked up everything," Sig said, shaking his head.

"So, I told 'im I was gon take my woman to Vegas for 'er birthday an I'll be back on the 1st. Before we left, I dropped Mr. Pepper's $50,000.00, and told 'im ta find out what's what, and he could arrange for me to turn myself in on the 4th."

With a surprised look on his face, Sig said, "Dog. You Crazy! You don't neva turn yo'self in to these folks."

"Oh, if he woulda blew some bullshit outta his head, I would've bounced faster than that red ghost gettin' ghost from Pac-Man.

"So, we went out west, and had a ball. Won some money, and lost even more. Then I jacked about $250,000.00 on Rodeo Drive when we hit Cali. My woman had a ball in Beverly Hills. She was in heaven, 'til the flight back home."

"What? You told her about the indictment?"

"Yeah. And she cried like a baby. But I had to prepare 'er for what was coming.

"I went to see Mr. Peppers April 2nd, and he told me they were charging me wit' the distribution of 4 kilos of cocaine. That phucked me up! I'm hitting niggas wit' no less than 10, and that's on consignment."

"You said niggas wit' an S? OH, you was moving some thangs," Sig said.

"I told you, I had a line. A hundred every month like clockwork."

"So you wasn't selling no individual birds?"

"Naw. That's why I figured it was old, and some bullshit. But dig this. My cousin, Rome, is one of them dudes that's always phuckin' up, so I'd just throw 'im yay, and if he knew somebody that wanted some, I'd let 'im make some chips like that too, you know.

"Man, one day this fool hits me like, 'I got somebody that wants four.' So I tell 'im ta come get 'em. This clown say 'would you take it to 'im? I'm out in Southfield and we goin' down to Atlanta for the Freaknik.' I'm like, I ain't gon sell my work and pay you. Hell naw! 'Come on Tay, I gotta go shopping and we 'spose ta leave in a few hours.' 'How much you tell 'im? 'Eighteen.'

"You shouldn't a did that shit." Sig said.

"He was 17 and I woulda had to give 'im some loot anyway, so I figured I might as well let 'im keep his clientele."

Shaking his head, Sig looked at me and said, "God sure does look out for fools and babies. Your lil cousin got lucky. What he doin' now?"

"My aunt said he's till hustling, and he's goin' down to Wayne State. Hopefully he'll be my lawyer when I get home."

Grinning, Sig asked me, "You ain't gonna leave da game alone when you hit da bricks?"

I looked at 'im and said, "You know shit don't stop!"

Chapter Four

"Gurl, that's Tay, let me call you back."

"Alright, tell 'im I said hi," Yolanda said before she hung up.

"Hey Baby," Tasha said purposely leaving out Landa's 'hi'.

"What's up wit' choo, my plump Princess?"

Smiling from ear to ear, Tasha said, "Nothing. Been wondering why you didn't call me back last night." Every since Tay had told her about them being locked down the first day he got there, she would worry whenever he didn't call when he'd say he would.

"By the time I finished puttin' in work on the chess board, it was time ta lock down."

"I saw Rome at school today. He gave me $500.00 for you, and said for you to send him a visiting form."

Surprised that his lil cousin gave Tash a half stack for him, Tay said, "Damn, he must be doin' aiight. 50 or even 100 wouldn't have surprised me, but 500! I'm impressed."

"He was probably trying to show off in front of Landa. He's kinda feeling her, as he's always saying.

"Oh, okay. So, how you feeling?"

"Me and the baby are fine. And no, I haven't been stressing." She knew that was gonna be his next question.

"Good girl. When you gonna find out what we having?"

In a whinny voice, Tasha said, "I told you that since you can't go with me that I wanna wait 'til I have it. Okay Daddy?"

"Aiight, Ma. So what's on your agenda for the day?"

"First I'm gonna get my hair done. Then I'm going over Mama's for dinner wit' her and Daddy. After that, I'm coming back home and go to bed so I can wake up early and get on the road to come see you."

"That sounds like a plan. Well Baby, I'm a let this dude use the phone. Tell Jason's faggot ass that he better have your shit whipped, and I'll see you tomorrow."

"Okay. I love you Daddy."

"Love you too. And be careful on the highway."

"I will. Bye Baby."

*****

Whenever Tasha would come back from seeing Dontae, she'd be exhausted, but, for some reason, she felt like going out. It might be from the pang of jealousy she felt when Dontae spoke to that officer, Ms. Massey. They just seemed a little too friendly to her. If the woman wasn't so attractive, Tasha wouldn't have thought of their exchange, but she knew her man. And, she knew that dark skin women turned him on. 'Then the bitch had the nerve to have, her own, shoulder length, silky black hair, and with a body like Lisa Raye's', Tasha thought. And one thing that Tasha was sure of was that women were easily drawn to Dontae. His 5'10" frame carried his 200 solid pounds perfectly. And his coca complexion attracted both the women that liked their men light or dark. Dontae was charismatic and his wavy ass hair made you instantly wanna rub his head. As

Tasha started dialing Trina's number, she decided that she was going to ask Dontae what was up wit' him and that bitch.

Tasha was looking through her closet for something to wear when Trina answered her telephone. "Hey Gurl," Trina said poppin' gum in Tasha's ear.

"Nothing. Looking through my mini Saks 5th for something to wear. And I know I can't fit shit in here, wit' my pregnant ass."

In a voice filled with disbelief, Trina said, "I know you ain't going out to intoxicate, and bounce Dontae's baby around tonight. He's gon kill you."

"No. I'm not gonna drink. But, I need to get out. You wanna hit Jewels tonight?"

"Bitch, you know it. You already hollered at Landa?"

"Naw. She told me Thursday when we were leaving school not to call her this weekend 'cause she'd be studying. So," in a singing voice, Tasha said, "it's just me and you."

"Well, that's cool with me, let me get dressed. What time you picking me up?"

"I'll be there between 9 and 9:30."

"All right, bye."

"Bye."

By the time Tasha pulled up to Trina's it was a quarter to ten. When Tasha hit the horn Trina came right out. It's the end of October and I bet she's damn near naked up under that coat, Tasha thought to herself as Trina opened the door and got into the car. "Let me guess. You wore the full length mink to attract the attention, but the real attention getter is underneath the coat," Tasha said, shaking her head.

With a fake appalled look, and a smile on her face, Trina said, "No. The mink keeps me warm, and you will see that I am dressed like a L-A-D-Y tonight."

"Well, excuse me."

"A bitch is excused. You must be dressed a little slutty," in an uppity voice Trina said. Then in an uppity voice, she continued, "up under that beaver."

"Shidd. For one, you know I never dress whorish. Two, I'm pregnant, and three, my man figures if the fur can keep the animals warm 24/7, then it will definitely keep me warm as I travel to and from my SL in the winter months."

As they rode, Trina told Tasha how the remarks she'd made to her some months back had made her make a self-evaluation. Trina told Tasha she no longer allowed men in the house and that she had been back in touch with Tone, going to visit him on a regular basis, and trying to get back into his good graces. Their heart to heart came to a halt when they pulled up to the valet in the parking lot at Jewels.

Trina said, "Damn! This muthaphucka looks like the showroom at the Detroit Auto Show."

"Girl, Detroit niggas get money, can dress and…"

"Can get some pussy if they mouthpiece is tight and we hittin' the Westin and not the Red Roof," Trina said finishing Tasha's sentence.

As soon as they entered the club, heads started turning. Donned in a champagne colored maternal Prada dress, with the Prada shoes to match, Tasha looked radiant. Her jet black hair with the blond streaks and highlights had a slight part down the middle and laid comfortably on her shoulders. At 5'4" her frame carried the extra weight beautifully, and if not for the little knot in her stomach, one would think she was just thick, not pregnant. And her peanut butter complexion was glowing.

Standing at 5'9", ultra thick, with sandy brown hair and emerald green eyes, Trina was truly a nice piece of eye candy. Her black Vera Wang dress accentuated her hips and round set-a-glass-on-it ass, and even made her C cups look like D's.

As they were making their way toward an empty table, they took in the roaming eyes of the men and the rolling eyes of the women in the room. The bar was full of women sitting down and men standing beside them with drinks in hand getting their mack on. The dance floor was packed with couples dancing to Mary J, featuring Method Man's *Love At First Sight*.

Once they sat down, Tasha said, "Between these lights and these niggas' wrists and hands, I'm a be blind."

"Well, you're doing your part too," Trina said, pointing to the rock on Tasha's left ring finger. Dontae had bought a three carat canary solitaire diamond ring the day before he was convicted. Her thoughts were broken when a man in black wool slacks with black Gucci loafers and a cream colored turtle neck approached their table and asked Trina if she would like to dance. Accepting, she looked at Tasha and said, "I'll be back to check on you in a minute."

"Girl, gon' and enjoy yourself. I'm strait."

As Tasha sat at the table looking at Trina get her groove on, the waitress approached with a drink in a large glass. Before she could finish saying that she can't drink alcohol the waitress said, "Its only orange juice. It's from the gentleman at the bar. He'd like to know if he can join you, so you can thank him personally." Tasha started to decline, but figured a little conversation won't hurt. She looked at him and nodded her head. When he stood and started toward the table the waitress tapped her shoulder and said, "Good choice," and left. Tasha wasn't so sure. He was about 6'2" with a bald head. His full beard meshed perfectly with his brown skin and thick eye brows. Wearing an Armani suit—although she wasn't sure of the color because of the lighting—and gators, he looked stunning to Tasha.

"Thank you for the drink," Tasha said, as he sat down.

In a deep baritone voice, he said, "You're welcome, but I thank you for allowing me to join you." Tasha just blushed and sat speechless. "My name is Alex," he said, extending his hand across the table.

Tasha noticed that his fingers were freshly manicured, but the pinkie ring that looked like it was a hall of mirrors was what really caught her attention. "Tasha," she said, as she lightly shook his hand.

"Well Tasha, it's a pleasure to make your acquaintance. And might I add that you look ravishing tonight. You're a gorgeous woman."

"Thank you. You're pretty easy on the eye's yourself." 'I'm flirting and I better stop,' Tasha thought to herself. "However, I do have a man that I'm deeply in love with, and I'm six months pregnant with his child."

Smiling and looking Tasha in her eye's he said, "The fact that you're pregnant was not lost on me, but I saw a beautiful woman that piqued my interest, and I'm thankful that her mans a fool."

"Excuse me!" Tasha said, looking a little thrown by his last statement.

"Well, a man must be a fool to allow his woman to attend a spot like this with her attractive friend instead of himself."

With an appalled look, Tasha said, "ALLOW!"

"When I say allow, I don't mean in a controlling manner. I mean, if you wanted to go out, why wouldn't he escort you? Surely, if he's your man, your best friend, and your confidant, you'd prefer to be with him instead of your girlfriend. But why he's not here isn't important. I'd like to know more about you."

During their conversation Tasha found out that Alex was 32, divorced, had no kids and owned a steel company. However, she knew that steel wasn't his only occupation. Tasha told him that she was 21 and that she was in her junior year at Wayne State University. She also told him that she wanted to be a lawyer, but she mainly kept him talking about himself. And she never mentioned that her man was locked up.

The conversation came to an end when Trina and Rome walked up. When Tasha tried to introduce Alex to them Rome just looked at him and his outstretched hand. Then he turned to Tasha and said, "My man told me to make sure you get home safely. Since I'm 'bout to leave I think I should walk you to your car. Where's your coat check ticket?"

Rather than taking the risk of seeming like she was enjoying her company she reached in her Prada bag and retrieved the ticket. When Rome and Trina went to get the coats, Alex asked, "Who was that?"

As Tasha stood, she said, "Must be my bodyguard."

"Well, since we were interrupted, can we finish our conversation over lunch? Dinner? Or the phone?"

"Alex, thanks for the drink, and your company, but I'm happily involved. Nice meeting you," she said, as she walked off.

Chapter Five

I had been on the yard for about an hour, but the cold weather chased me back to the unit on the ten minute move. Plus the football games had kicked off, so my weekend activity would consist of me sitting in the sports TV room all day. When I walked pass the office in route to the TV room I heard Ms. Massey call my name.

When I walked in the office I said, "What's up Monique?"

In the seven months that I had been there me and her had become close. She used to always talk about Tash being so small and say, "Thick women must scare me." Eventually I told her that women with ass like hers usually can't take dick like mine. And from that point on we would constantly flirt, and have no holds barred conversations.

"Nothing," she said, as she filed her nails.

"What's on your mind?" I asked her.

"You. And I was wondering why all your visits lately have been from the cute fella you say is your cousin, and not the little girl you claim is grown."

"Oh, my cousin is cute to you huh?"

"Are you jealous?"

"A little," I lied.

"He's cute, but I only dig one Manning. So, where's girlie?"

"It's getting close to that time and I don't want 'er on the highway. She'll be down here in a couple of weeks for Christmas. Then she'll come after she has the baby."

"Oh. I thought the chicken had flew the coop."

"Naw," I said, shaking my head.

Looking at my eyes she said, "You gon mess around and lose your visits if you keep smoking that stuff. Mr. Langford is a bad influence on you. That's why I won't give you none. You keep bad company."

"I don't wanna hear that shit."

She looked up at me and said, "You beta watch your mouth."

"I ain't beta watch shit." She looked around me into the hall when she busted out laughing. "You don't give me none 'cause you don't wanna be strung out. I know you ain't worried 'bout losing this lil job. I was serious when I said you can quit. Being my woman can be more profitable anyway."

"And I was serious when I told you that I like my job, and that I ain't playing second to Tasha or no other bitch," she said, looking at me and rolling her neck like only a sistah can.

"Girl you beta watch your mouth."

"I ain't beta watch shit," she smartly responded, and pursed her lips together in a smirk.

*****

Me and my bunky, Yahmo, had become real tight. He was the only person that I talked to about Monique. Sig was my main man, but me and Yahmo vibed more when strictly on some playa shit. However, we were all on the same page when money was the topic.

And I knew today was no different when he came in the room with a Swisher Sweet and a box of Black and Milds.

When he sat down I grabbed the box of Blacks, opened them and proceeded to freak one. He started to breakdown the weed, then he stopped and sat back in the chair, looked at me and said, "When we gon' start gettin' this money in here? I know we gon' get it on the bricks, but it's time to live off the land, now."

"Shid, what choo wanna do?"

Once he saw that I was interested, and he had my attention he started rolling the blunt. "I wanna get some boy, but I don't have the resources," he told me.

"Man, explain to me how you were plugged the way you were, didn't tell, and none of your people holla at choo! You can't even get a gram of boy?" I asked, with a look of bewilderment on my face.

"I know it seems strange, but you'd have to be involved to understand," he said, as he hit the blunt and passed it to me.

I took a hit and said, "I know you ain't hurting fa nothin', but DAMN! I don't neva hear you say you talked to your mans or nothin'."

"We ain't mans. We're loyal business associates. And they don't holla at nobody that's locked down."

"Damn! That's some helluva shit!"

"Like, I got mad love fa you. You my mans! But when I leave in three more years I'm a leave you a number. Don't call me until you get home, and you won't hear from me either."

"Strait up?"

"Yup. But you won't give a phuck, trust me. But what's up now?"

"My lil cousin is in the mix, so I'll holla at 'im and we'll put this shit on the flo'"

"Aiight. When you ready let me know. I already got a mule. We'll just pay 'im in stamps. It'll be cheaper like that."

"Bet. Nah pass the weed nigga."

*****

Whenever I got high I felt like playing chess, and I was on my way to find a victim when me and Monique made eye contact. She nodded her head toward **The Middle**, and from the look on her face I knew she needed to talk to me.

The Middle was where the Unit Manager, Case Manager's and the secretaries' offices were. It was located between the adjoining units. On the weekends, after four, all the administrators were gone home and the officers would go back there and just kick it.

I went and acted like I was on the phone. When I heard the door slam I waited, cause every eye in the unit followed that fat ass thru the door. After a minute or so I hung up the phone and went back there. She locked the door behind me and we went into the bathroom.

I looked at her and said, "What's up Baby? What's on your mind?"

Shaking her head, she passed me a six pack of grape bubble gum and said, "Nothing. Just wanted to give you some of your favorite gum and holla at choo before I go on vacation."

"Starting when? And how long you gon' be gone?"

"Today is my last day, and I'll be off for three weeks."

"Damn! So I won't see you for Christmas, or New Years huh?"

"Nope. You gon miss me?"

"Hell yeah! Come here." I grabbed her around her waist, pulled her toward me, and for the first time we kissed. The way she responded lessened the doubt I had when she told me she'd been celibate for the past two years. I went from grabbing her voluptuous ass to massaging her D cup titties to trying to take that damn utility belt off. From the way she was massaging my dick I thought she was going to finally give me the goods. Then all of a sudden she pulled away from me.

"Dontae, I can't do this right now. Please don't be mad at me," she said, as she began to fix her uniform.

To hide the look of disappointment that I'm sure my face displayed, I hugged her and whispered in her ear, "Baby its aiight. I ain't trippin'."

She pulled back a little bit and asked me, "Are you sure? I'm not trying to tease you."

"Yeah, I'm sure," I said. "But he's pissed!" I said, pointing to the bulge in my pants, and we both started laughing.

Before I left to go get me some freak books and put my "Do Not Disturb" sign in the window of my door, I got me a good bye kiss and gave her Rome's number. I told her to call him on Christmas, then again the day before New Year's Eve.

*****

When I finished shaving and taking a shower I laid back in my bunk and continued to read "Thugs and the Women Who Love Them" by Wahida Clark. As soon as I started to really get into it, I heard them call my name for a visit over the loud speaker. I got up, got dressed, brushed my teeth again and went to get my pass.

It had been over a month since the last time I had seen my Pooh. When I saw her I lit up. "C'mere you," I said with my arms spread apart. We kissed so long and passionately that the guard came and broke it up.

"What's up my man?" I greeted my cousin, as I gave him a quick hug.

"Same ole shit. Getting that money and trying to keep good grades," he said, as we all sat down.

"Ask 'im," Tash said, looking at Rome smiling.

"Ask me what?"

"What choo gon' do wit' da Caddy?" Rome asked me.

"The notes wit' the insurance is damn near $900 a month. Can you handle that?"

"Easily," he said, looking at me like I was crazy.

"What's your grades like?"

"First semester I had a 2.8."

"That ain't good. That's just average. Dig, give Tash 10 and take over the note. If you finish the year wit' a 3.0 or better you get a 10 gee rebate."

"Bet. Tasha I'll give you that when we get back so I can get those keys."

"So how have you been? I been missing you like crazy," I said, as I turned my attention back to my Pooh.

"Tired and cranky. I want choo home yesterday and the day before that and the day..."

"Pooh don't do that to yourself. It could be much worse. Wit' my good time and the drug program, that 8 don't look bad at all," I said, planting small kisses on her forehead.

"How bad is not bad? And don't tell me how many years. I wanna know what year you'll be home."

"Around March of 2001."

"Fa real! Damn I was thinking it was going to be 03 or 04. I think we should eat to celebrate. What choo want?"

"It don't matter sexy. Whatever you want me to have is fine."

"Okay, you going to eat wit' me then. Rome you want something?"

"Uh, just bring me some kind of fruit juice please."

"Alright, I'll be back," she said, and gave me a quick kiss before she left.

I immediately used that time to kick it with Rome about a couple of things that I needed him to do for me.

"Aiight nigga, what's on yo mind? I can tell you wanna kick it 'bout somethin'," Rome said, and leaned forward so we didn't have to talk too loud.

Making sure that Tash was busy at the microwave I said, "Ain't no doubt. You got a hook up on the boy?"

"Yeah. My mans be phuckin' wit' it. Why? What's up?"

"As long as it's the strong I'm a need you to get it fa me."

"That ain't shit."

"And I need a chick about 35 or 36 to come see my mans."

"Hell, that's even easier. Anything else?"

"Yeah. I gave a female friend your cell number, and yes she's off limits. Anyway, she's gon' call you on Christmas and the day before New Year's Eve; and you'll have somethin' for 'er."

"What?" He asked with a look of confusion on his face.

"I don't know yet. I'll call and let choo know in the next day or two."

"Aiight."

Tash came back, and while she fed me, and herself, we talked and reminisced. We talked about everything from her grades, which were excellent, to how she had to start the eviction process on a few of the tenants that were living in some of our houses. At the end of the visit, after we finished kissing, she said, "I'll see you next week for Christmas. I wish you could come home and fuck me into labor." That statement gave me an instant erection.

As they were leaving out of the visiting room I told Rome, "I want choo to ride up here wit' my Pooh next week. Tell Aunt Tina I said hi, and I'll call you tomorrow 'bout that." To all of which he said, "Okay." Being nosey, Tash wanted to know what 'That' was.

Chapter Six

"Damn girl, you got some good ass pussy, wit' some superb skills," Rome told Landa, after their second sexual episode of the morning.

"Well why in the hell you be giving this muthaphucka to other bitches?" She asked him, while gently tugging on his flaccid manhood. "And you can't lie, cause Trina saw you at the Palladium wit' some bitch. We was over Tasha's the other day and she was like, 'I saw Rome's sexy ass last night at the Palladium wit' some trick. Now that he's matured I might let him be the first man in "97" to get in these jeans. And if it's like that he'll be the only one until Tone comes home.' I wanted to tell 'er ass that me and you are good friends, and you're off limits."

"So we're only good friends, huh?"

"I don't know, you tell me," Landa said, rolling her eyes.

Sitting up on his elbows, Rome said, "Shid, you got keys to my crib, got clothes in the closet, know where the money is, but unlike Jay-Z, I know ya name."

"Well, I know how to ride nice dick, know how to work my hips, and the head is priceless, and unlike the woman Mr. Carter was talking to in the song, I didn't save the merits for carats. Or ask you to wife me and buy me nice whips, but if I'm your woman, I'm demanding monogamy."

Rome sat up and looked Landa in her eyes and said, "Baby you got that. Just hold me down and I'll always love you like you deserve to be loved."

"Did I hear the word **love** come out of your mouth, in reference to your feelings about me?" Landa asked Rome, and bit down on her lower lip.

"You heard right. We been phuckin' 'round since October. It's just that shit became official today."

"I love you too Boo. And I can't wait to see what I get next March 24th for our one year anniversary."

"Let me find out that you're using me."

She whispered in his ear, "I am, for the dick, but not the money."

*****

As soon as Rome finished cooking up, cutting and bagging the work for his spots the phone rang. "What." After a brief pause he pressed 5.

"What's up young fool," Tay said.

"Shit. I got three hoes here that just finished cooking, and I'm 'bout to take a shower and go drop they asses off. What's up wit' choo?"

"Doing what must be done. Other than that, nothing. I really need to talk to the love of your life. She there?" Tay asked.

"Damn, news travels fast."

"As soon as Tash and Lil Tay came in the visiting room last week she started yappin' 'er gums. 'My lil brother and my best friend are in love, and my other best friend is a little jealous.' I already knew who she was talking about. I wasn't surprised either, cause you always had a crush on Landa, but I was shocked you hadn't knocked off Trina's thick freak ass."

With his voice full of excitement, Rome said, "Man, I wanted to, but neva got 'round to it. Now it's too late, cause I value, and I'm honoring my relationship."

"I feel you. Oh well, phuck it."

"Hit me on da cell at 'bout 3. Landa will be wit' me. I'm goin' to get 'er from school, then we goin' to get Lil Tay so Tasha can study. We gon' shoot to Northland."

"That's perfect. You know Tash' birthday is in two days. Have Landa pick 'er out a few fits, then shoot to Greenfield Plaza and get 'er a icy ankle bracelet for me. Whateva the ticket is let me know and I'll shoot it to you."

"Aiight my man I'll…"

Tay cut Rome off before he could finish. "Oh, holla at cha mans too."

"Oh, aiight. I'll holla at choo."

"Much love."

"Much."

After Rome hung up he took a shower, got dressed, grabbed the work, hopped in his Escort and bounced.

When he pulled up in front of his ounce spot on Cortland, a little dude about 16 came to the car carrying two brown paper bags. As soon as he got in Rome pulled off. "Lil Tee, what's the word?" Rome asked his little soldier, and gave him some dap.

"Its one O left, and it'll probably be gone by the time I get back. The drought done hit and we was the only ones wit' da bomb. I ain't gon' lie O.G., I ain't short the grams, or cut the work, cause we got a rep to uphold, but I upped the price from seven to nine."

Not mad at all, Rome said, "This what we gon' do. The drought ain't gonna affect us. Take these O's." Rome reached in the backseat and handed Lil Tee the bag that had the O's bagged up. "Take 'em in and start pushing 'em fa $1,200.00. I'm a get Teddy, he works my rock spot, I'm gon' bring 'im over here to move da O's. I need you to do the rocks, cause we gon' flood da rock spot and just keep the O spot afloat."

"Aiight. What's my ticket gon' be?"

"I'll let choo know when I get back, but it'll be sweet."

The house sat four houses from the corner. Rome watched Lil Tee until he went in, then he pulled off with the .45 in his lap, listening to Biggie's '*Ready to Die*.'

Rome had been hustling good for about a year and a half, but this was the time he'd been waiting for. Dontae told him a few months ago that when the drought hits he was gonna make his pockets heavy.

When he got indicted he shut his operation down, fearing that he was being watched, so Rome knew he could get his hands on some work. Rome didn't know how much Tay had, but he knew his cousin had it. When he pulled up in front of his spot on Dakota, off of Woodward Ave. he honked his horn. A dark skin dude about 23 came out the house carrying a blue Nike gym bag. When he got in the car Rome asked him, "You got anymore work in the house?"

"Nope. They ate that shit up a few hours ago." When Rome pulled off Teddy threw the bag on the floor in the backseat and continued talking. "Fiends from everywhere was coming thru cause everybody else is out, or they shit little as hell."

"Well, my people said we might be able to stay above water. I'm a take you on Cortland and let you push O's. I just dropped 80 over there."

"That'll work. But the work is so good we could push 'em fa $1500."

"Ain't no need to squeeze 'em unless we get squoze. Our spots boom, our works da bomb, and we fair. That's how you do business."

"I feel you," Teddy replied.

When they pulled up on Cortland, Rome told Teddy, "Tell Shorty I said to come on, and leave you all the money he made off the sack. I'll holla at choo in the morning if I can get some mo' yay."

"Aiight. I'll holla at choo."

Luckily tomorrow was Friday, so Rome could go see Tay. After Lil Tee gets the last brick an a half in rocks he'll be out of yay like every other unplugged dealer. However, when he came back from Ohio, Rome had a feeling he wasn't going to be like the average dealer.

"Let's roll O.G.," Tee said, as he closed the door. "I sold that last O, fa $1200.00 of course, like you said."

"Put that in ya pocket," Rome told him.

"I knew you was gon' say that, so I split the $1200 wit' my dog that sit in there wit' me."

"That's cool. Where he at? I ain't see 'im come out da house," Rome asked, as he made a right on Dexter.

"He went out the back door. I told 'im I'll holla at 'im when I come back over there."

"Okay. Well dig, I got a brick and a half, and it's cut up in nice size rocks. Just pump 'em."

"Aiight O.G."

*****

After Rome dropped Lil Tee off he went and picked up Landa. "Hey Baby. How was school today?" He asked her, as he leaned over and gave her a long passionate kiss.

"Not as good as that kiss, but much better than riding in this. I hate this car. I hope we ain't goin' shopping in this."

"Naw. You can take the Caddy."

Pissed off, Landa put her hand on her hip as she leaned on the door, and asked, "Oh, you ain't going wit' us?"

"Baby I can't. Fa real, I got some shit I gotta do, then I gotta get some rest cause I have to go see Dontae tomorrow."

Landa knew it was serious when he said Tay's whole name, so she softened up. "Okay. Well be home at seven so we can eat dinner together and I can put choo to bed properly," she said, as she was rubbing the back of his neck.

When they made it back to Rome's apartment, he pulled in next to his Caddy. After he gave her a few knots out of the Nike bag he told her what Tay wanted her to do for Tasha, gave her a kiss, told her he loved her and then waited until she pulled off. Then he grabbed the bags and went into the apartment.

*****

Rome sat in the visiting room awaiting his cousin. Last night, today seemed like it wasn't ever going to come. He and Landa made love all night, and for the first time she went to sleep, and he was wide awake. Now it seemed like Tay was taking forever. While he was heating up his sandwiches he saw Tay walk in and start talking to the few people there, and their visitors like he was running for president. He grabbed his sandwiches out of the mic, and the other snacks and juices he'd bought, then headed toward Tay. As he sat the food down and embraced Tay, he said, "Damn you're popular."

With his arms spread apart in a **'What Can I Say'** stance, and a cool expression on his face, Tay said, "Well you know I'm a people person. It's only the authorities that I don't get along wit'." Rome nodded his head in agreement. "Now, what's goin' on wit' choo? I know you ain't just popped up down here cause you missed me."

"Oh yeah, I'm on some business shit."

"I hope its business and not bullshit."

"Man da drought done hit, and I…"

"Ain't got no work," Tay said, finishing his sentence.

"Nope." Rome said, shaking his head and looking at him.

"But you know the Don got some?"

"Yup." He answered, nodding his head and smiling.

"Okay, what choo want me to give you?" Tay asked.

Surprisingly he told Tay, "I don't want choo ta give me nothin'. I got $120,000 that I wanna spend."

"Oh, you have grown up a lil bit."

"I told choo that I don't be phuckin' up no mo'. I been coppin' two and three bricks. I got a few spots, but my weight clientele eats that lil shit up. When I heard that yay was scarce I took the lil change I had and bought the three hoes I was talkin' 'bout yesterday, fa 20 apiece."

"And what choo do wit' 'em?" Tay asked.

"Well, I was able to get a extra 18 off of every 36, so I just split 'em up and put one in my rock spot and the other half in my O spot, and pushin' 'em fa $1,200."

Tay's face wrinkled up in a look of confusion. "So you mean ta tell me that you gave your workers a ticket in oppose to a salary?"

"Hmm Hm."

"Nigga, you backwards as phuck! What kinda hustling you doing?" Tay asked his cousin.

While he was sitting there looking crazy Tay said, "First of all, ain't nothin' wrong wit' showing love, but those are your spots. They work for you. You put 'em on salary. And second of all, if it's a drought and you only got 3 slabs, you gotta do 'em in all rocks baby. The drought is for niggas that got work ta come all the way up. Cats like you that's gettin' a brick or two needs to milk what he can out of the ones he has when the drought hits. Cause the dudes like me, that the drought don't apply to, ain't selling no mo' bricks 'til it's over. I got rock spots, and I can get you eights for between $3500 and $4000. It all depends on the relationship."

"I'm feeling you," Rome said, nodding his head.

"See, this is the time that dudes that's gettin' eights and quarters, and ain't stacking, end up having to have somebody give 'em an O or two to get on they feet when the drought blows over."

Still nodding his head, Rome said, "I got choo."

"You don't be sitting here lecturing nobody."

Tay and Rome were so enthralled in their conversation that Tay didn't even see Monique walk up. "Hey. How you doing Ms. Massey? This is my cousin Jerome. I was just telling 'im how important it is for 'im to graduate from college."

"How you doing?" Monique asked, as she extended her hand to Rome.

With his eyes going from her wrist to his cousin, he smiled and said, "I'm aiight."

"That's good," she replied. Then she looked at Tay and said, "Enjoy your visit, I'll see you later Mr. Manning."

"Aiight."

"Nice meeting you," she told Rome, as she walked off.

"So that's the recipient of the seven carat tennis bracelet, and the five dozen roses?" Rome asked, looking at Tay.

"Yeah, that's my girl there."

"You fucking the C.O. huh?" Rome said, sounding like Juve.

"Naw, she ain't gave me no pussy yet, but we be kicking it."

He told Rome about how he and Monique started kicking it and how he was starting to feel her more than he probably should. Then he told him about the killing him and his bunky were making off the boy that Rome was getting for him, and that led back to their initial topic.

"So what you gon' give dem' thangs to me fa, so I can be on da bricks killin' 'em?"

"Look," Tay began, "do not broadcast that you got work. Niggas' that ask, just tell 'em you can see if ya mans is still right and play like you're the middle man. Turn the O spot into a rock spot and bust open a few more. Take Tash $85,000, and she'll give you 10. You'll still owe me 85. Now go get money young nigga."

Smiling like a kid on Christmas, Rome hugged Tay and said, "Good lookin' out, fa real. By the time you come home we gon' be able to go legit."

Tay looked his little cousin in the eyes and said, "Just be careful. When I come home we gon' take shit to a whole notha level."

Chapter Seven

Tasha, Trina, and Landa were sitting in the living room at Tasha's house having lunch. It had been a long time since all three of them had been together. Between school and Rome, Landa had really been out of the mix. Trina had been hired as the bank manager at Comerica Bank on Meyers and Six Mile. Tasha had her hands full. She was a mommy, a full time student, going to see Dontae at least twice a month, and still had to conduct his business transactions. In the midst of a Trina joke the doorbell rang.

"That's probably my baby. I'll get it," Landa said, as she got up to answer the door. When she walked back into the living room she was carrying two dozens of white roses. With a smile on her face, Landa said, "These are for you Ms. Foster."

"Whose bed have you been in?" Trina asked.

Taken aback, Tasha looked at Trina and said, "Mine! And the only other occupant is my son."

Handing Tasha the roses Landa said, "Well, somebody is feeling you."

As she started to remove the card that was attached, in unison, Trina and Landa said, "Bitch! Read it out loud."

Laughing, she looked at them and started reading to herself. Then she said, "Listen to this: Sorry to invade your private space, but it's time to resume the conversation that we started. You can reach me at 555-1975. Arrangements have already been made. Alex."

Trina stood with her mouth wide open, and with a questioning look on her face, she said, "Damn girl, how do he know where you live?"

Shaking her head Tasha said, "I haven't the slightest idea."

Looking from Trina to Tasha, Landa asked, "Who the phuck is Alex? Bitch you been creeping and didn't tell me?"

"No. I met him last year when me and Trina went out, and I haven't heard from, or seen him since."

"The question is, are you going to call him?" Trina asked.

With a skeptical look on her face Landa said, "You bet not. He might want more than conversation."

"You know he does. He done hunted her ass down," Trina said, looking at Landa wit' the "duh" look.

"I might call to resume our conversation, but he ain't gettin' no booty."

With the look of a parent warning their child, Landa pointed her finger at Tasha and said, "You done waited until you're 22 years old to start playing with fire. Girl you know damn well that taking that man up on his offer is an invitation by you as well. Regardless of what you do I'm on your side, but if you don't want to start nothin', I'd advise you to throw that number away."

The following day, after Tasha had put Lil Tay down for his nap, she called Alex. "Hello, Bryant Steel. May I help you?"

Tasha was about to hang up, figuring that she had dialed the wrong number, but then she remembered that he owned a steel company. "Yes, may I speak to Alex please?"

"I'm sorry, but Mr. Bryant isn't in. May I take a message?"

"Just tell 'im that Ratasha called."

"Oh! Ms. Foster?"

A mixture of shock and uneasiness shot thru Tasha, "Yes," she said, as she wondered how he had accumulated so much information about her.

"Mr. Bryant would like to know if you'll be free for dinner tonight. Or breakfast, lunch, or dinner tomorrow?"

"Tell him I said that dinner tomorrow will be fine."

"Confirmed. The driver will be to pick you up at 7:30 p.m."

"Okay. Thank you."

*****

Tasha and Landa were on their way to Fishbones. Tasha had a meeting with a man about some land that Dontae was interested in. It had been a couple of weeks since the last time that they had talked, and Tasha was giving Landa the rundown on Alex, and their date.

"So how did he find out where you live?"

"When I asked him that, he told me that he knew my name and what school I attended, so attaining the information that he needed was easy."

"Well damn! Tell me how the date with Mr. Resourceful went."

"Girrrl! He sent his driver to pick me up in a steel gray 600."

"Damn! He's playing wit' Tonka toys," Landa said, and then raised her hand to give Tasha a hi-five.

"Oh, it don't stop there. Do you know where dinner was?"

"Phuck the guessing games. Bitch tell me what happened."

"On his hundred foot yacht…"

Hi-fiving Tasha again and covering her mouth with her hand, Landa yelled, "No it wasn't!"

"Oh yes it was. Landa, he had his chef prepare some exquisite shit that I can't even pronounce. And as the pianist played my request, we sailed and ate dinner by candle light in between the United States and Canada."

"Tasha you better stay away from his resourceful ass." Fanning herself and shaking her head, Landa whispered, "Tasha did you fuck him?"

"I'll admit that things did get heated, but I couldn't do that to Tay. Alex said he understood, and was a perfect gentleman for the remainder of the night."

"I know he's wondering where your so-called man is."

"Probably, but ain't no questions been asked, therefore, ain't no answers been given."

"I know that's right. So, have you seen him again?" Landa asked.

"Naw, but we've talked on the phone a few times. He always asks when he can see me again, but I told him that now is not a good time. I really enjoy talking to him. He told me that patience made him successful, and he believes it'll also make him happy."

Wiping the fake sweat from her forehead, Landa said, "You better cut all lines of communication with him. He sounds dangerous."

Chapter Eight

Just like Tay told him, Rome's pockets had gotten heavy during that drought. He made more money than he had ever made. Even though the hook up from Tay only lasted a few months, he was in a position to make major moves. When his initial connect got back on, he couldn't really supply Rome like he wanted too. Over the last few months Rome was only able to really keep his rock houses flooded, cause the cats who wanted weight wanted weight. He wasn't losing money, but he was missing money, and getting money had become his vice. And like all addicts, he needed to feed his habit.

As him and his mans, Junior, who he grew up with, were heading to Ford Field to see the Lions play their annual Thanksgiving Day game, Rome kicked it with his best friend. "Man you been gon' fa three years. I'm happy as hell that you're home. Wit' Tay gon' I ain't have nobody out here that I could count on, and trust."

"Niggas' that was just gettin' to MTU used to be like, 'ya mans out there eating." Rome just smiled. "I knew shit had to be aiight, cause you neva sent me less than a few yards. But last month when I came home, and you dropped me 20 stacks, I was like damn, my man done came up."

"Shit should be better. I can't get the hook-up like I need. I gotta go shopping. When can you travel?"

"Once I report, on the first, I'm free till after the New Year. My P.O., Mr. Robinson is cool as hell. So after the first let's do this."

After they left the game Rome dropped Junior at his mother's house, then he headed to Landa's mothers house for Thanksgiving dinner. Everything was going like he wanted it too. The money was rolling in, him and Landa's relationship was solid, and he'd have a real plug real soon.

*****

"Damn Rome, when I left the streets we was messing wit' high class hood rats. Now Landa is your woman," Junior said from the backseat.

Rome glanced behind him smiling and said, "Well, I was coming up and needed somebody to represent me, so I laid my mack down on 'er."

"Shut up," Landa said, as she playfully punched Rome in the side. "Junior, did he tell you how I made him turn in his whore card and put on a mink leash?"

Laughing, Junior said, "You know, I think he forgot to mention how it really went down." Then they all busted out laughing.

When they arrived at Metro Airport, Landa asked Rome, "How long you gon' be gone Baby?"

Rome gave her a hug and a kiss, and told her he'd see her in about a week. After they checked their luggage, they headed toward the gate they were directed to. Once they boarded the plane, they kicked back in the plush leather first class seats. As they taxied down the runway, Rome sipped his Cognac, and said "Tonight when we get there we have to hit a spot where the heavy hitters hang. It has to be a spot that's mainly frequented by Mexicans, but blacks hang there too."

"Why Mexicans?" Junior asked.

"Cause they're the ones with all the work in Cali. Don't get me wrong, niggas' got it too, but not like the Mexicans. I was out there about a year ago phuckin' wit' this lil black chick name Brook. One night, during pillow talk, she put me up on a lot of shit.

Her brothers were in da game, and her man got Buck Rogers numbers in da Fed joint. She said once dude started really getting money, he had to deal wit' the Mexicans. And you know hoes always know what's going on when they're around that lifestyle."

When their plane landed at LAX they retrieved their luggage and headed to Hertz car rental. Rome rented a pearl white Caddy El-dog. "You kike these Caddy's don't choo." Junior stated, as they rode to the hotel.

"Man, I'm a get my woman one too. These muthaphuckas' ride. When I go holla at Tray I just slap a CD in and float down to that bitch. It feels like you're riding on air."

"When is that nigga coming home?"

"He'll probably hit the halfway house in August of 2001. Ain't but 26 days left in this year, so he got about three left."

"Oh, that ain't shit. He'll be touching down before he knows it."

"Dog, that fool phuckin' wit' a cold ass officer up there, and he moving that boy like Frank Wizzite."

"I ain't surprised. Since we was little Tay kept hoes and was doing shit to keep money in his pocket. Ain't no telling how big he'd be if Elijah hadn't gotten killed. He was a gangsta fa real!"

Rome looked over at Junior and said, "Shid! He wouldn't have let Tay get in da game. Tay used to hustle on the low-low. Elijah woulda beat Tay's ass if he knew he was selling rocks. He wanted Tay in school."

"Oh, I thought he was schooling Tay."

"Hell naw!"

After Rome and Junior checked into their hotel, they went to their rooms and laid down. By 10:00 p.m. they were up, dressed, and down at the front desk talking to the clerks. One was a black woman in her early thirties and the white girl was about the same age.

"Can you ladies recommend a nice spot that's jumpin' on a Thursday night?" Rome asked them.

"It depends on the type of crowd yall wanna mingle with."

Looking both men up and down, the black lady said, "Cindy, I can already tell where they wanna hang out."

Junior glanced at her name tag, then looked at the woman and asked, "So where do we wanna hang, Carol?"

"Where the ballers ball, cause it's crawling wit' women looking for men like yall."

Smiling at her, Rome said, "Actually, I'm not in search of women. I'm from Detroit, and other than blacks, it's populated with Chaldeans and Latinos. I'm about to open a club in an interracial area and I'd like to visit some clubs like that."

"Oh, there's quite a few of those clubs," Cindy said, smiling at Rome.

They got the names and directions to some of the clubs and left. While they were riding, Junior said, "Cindy is a sexy lil white bitch, and her eyes were constantly lingering on you. You might have to knock 'er off."

"Yeah, I noticed that too. I'm a see what's up. If for nothing else, for a discount and a nut, yunno."

"Ain't no doubt. They all serve a purpose. But what's up wit' some trees? We're rolling through the land of the sticky icky."

"You know I only smoke every blue moon, but I' m sure we'll be able to get some in the club."

After riding for about 45 minutes they found Club Paradise. "Damn! It ain't nothin' but bad ass hoes in this spot. This is the kind of place that makes married men wish they'd never done that dumb shit."

"Yeah, but fuck the wrong one and you'll get that shit that'll make you wish you'd never done that dumb ass shit," Rome said.

Laughing, Junior gave Rome a play and said, "True dat, but I'm 'bout to interact tonight. For business purposes of course."

"Well let's interact."

They both hit the dance floor and danced with several beauties. After six straight songs Rome went to the bar and ordered a Corona wit' lime. He didn't want to do any heavy drinking, being in an unfamiliar setting. At about 3:00 a.m. they headed back to the room.

"That spot was strictly for partying," Junior said, as they rode back to the hotel.

"We got a few more days' to play in the night life, but tomorrow we hittin' some hoods."

"Just let me get some zees and I'll be wit' whateva," Junior told Rome.

When they entered the hotel lobby, Cindy was at the desk filing some papers. Rome said, "I'll holla at choo tomorrow. I'm 'bout to phuck wit' her fa a minute."

*****

The trip to Cali turned out to be more of a vacation than a business trip. He met a few cats, but no one that was talking what he wanted to hear. He discovered that he needed an inside track in order to plug in with the Mexicans. If not for his urge to smoke, he would have never met Jorge. Cindy introduced them when he asked her who had some potent weed. As it turned out, Jorge had all the seedless sticky you wanted. He claimed that he didn't indulge in yay, but Rome figured if he dealt with him long enough, other doors might open up. After the New Year he'd hit Texas or Florida, but meeting Jorge did make the trip worth being made.

Chapter Nine

When I came from my visit, I went in the office to turn my pass in. "What's wrong?" Monique asked. "Didn't you enjoy your visit?"

"I always enjoy my visits. I just got some shit on my mind," I told her.

"You know I'm here to listen, console, and offer the best advice that I can. Dontae, don't shut me out."

"It's just some shit I noticed today."

"What? You and Tasha having problems?"

"We ain't having problems, but something ain't right. I've been wit' her since she was 15, she turned 23 last week, so you know I know 'er. And she's picked up some characteristics that are within my realm, but not consistent wit' my ways. It's showing in her demeanor, and conversation."

"In other words, you think she's messin' around? And not wit some average Joe. Someone on your level."

Nodding my head, I said, "Pretty much."

"And that scares you? That's why you look like you lost your best friend?"

"Naw. The only thing that scares me is being broke. As long as Tash takes care of business, we cool. Regardless of what she does, I won't be in here more miserable because of it."

"Well, why the solemn look?"

"I was looking at my son today, and he looks just like my brother."

Looking surprised, Monique said, "I didn't know you had a brother."

"I did. He got killed when I was 15. Two years after our mother passed away with cancer."

"He was older than you?"

"Yeah, he had me by four years. When my mother died, we went to live wit' my aunt and my cousin Rome."

"The one that comes to see you?"

"Yeah, that's the one. But Elijah…"

"Sorry to cut you off, but Elijah is your brother?" She asked.

"Hmm hm. He was wild as hell! Stayed in the streets gettin' paid. By the time he turned 18 he had his own house, car and a lot of money. But if he caught me on the block serving fiends, I'd hafta run, but to no avail. He'd catch me and punish my legs and arms," I said, smiling as I thought back. "He was on some 'do as I say, not as I do' shit. And my son looks just like 'im. I was on the visit thinking about my brother, and my situation, knowing if he was alive that I wouldn't be in here."

"What happened? How'd he get killed?"

"One day I was at this store and had a knot of money. Some older cats saw it, slapped me upside my head and took it. I was too scared ta go tell Elijah cause I thought he was gon ask me where I got the money from.

"So, one day we was riding down Seven Mile on our way to Northland. That's the mall. He was taking me to get the new Jordan's. Then, in front of the this store called *Babbies*, stood them two niggas, drinking forties, and I got mad, just seein' 'em, and blurted out, "There go them niggas who robbed me." My brother was like, 'WHAT? WHERE?' "When I pointed them out he bust'd a U-turn in the middle of Seven Mile and jumped out. I knew he didn't have a gun on 'im when he started beatin' the shit outta one 'em niggas'. Then, before I knew it, the other cat had whipped his burner out and shot my brother in the back of his head."

Monique put her hand to her chest and said, "Oh baby, you saw that!"

"Yup. I saw that nigga do my brother." An as I looked into her watering eyes, I said, "And I'll never forget his face, or that day, for the rest of my life."

Monique just sat at the desk, staring at me, and I was quiet as well. Then she said, "Meet me in the middle."

I figured that she wanted to talk some more, and maybe hug and kiss me, which, at the moment, I needed. When I walked back there I headed toward the bathroom and she locked the door. When she came in I noticed that she had taken off that damn utility belt. I turned and saw it lying next to the toilet. As soon as I turned back around, I started to ask her a question, but she put her arms around my neck, and began to kiss me with a hunger that I thought only inmates experienced. Our tongues danced, and my hands caressed every part of her. Then I pulled back and said, "This is some I-wanna-give-you-some-pussy kissing."

Looking me in my eyes, she said, "I would like the conditions to be different, but I want it, and you want it, so I'ma give it to you."

I turned her around and started kissing her on her neck as I unfastened her pants. As I used my hands to push them down, she started switching in place to assist me. When they reached her ankles, she stepped out of one leg. I placed my right hand between her shoulders, like a running back following his blocks. She bent over and put one hand on the sink. With her free hand, she reached back, grabbed my hard tool, and guided it toward her love tunnel.

Once I felt the warmth and wetness of her, I slowly slid all the way in her. She gasped! I just stood there for about five seconds absorbing the moisture of that love hole. Then I slowly started to stroke, but by the time I started to pick up the pace, I felt myself ready to erupt, so I pulled out.

She turned around and looked at me and said, "Boo, I know you want it to last, but you gotta come on." I put the head back in and rolled my hips a few times then rode up in there. After 5 or 6 strokes, I felt my legs weakening and I shot off. The head was tender, but I kept trying to take short strokes cause I felt like I was in heaven and didn't want to return to hell. Monique stood up and reached her arms up and pulled me to her. She gave me a brief kiss, then said, "I'd like to cuddle and all that good stuff too, but we gotta go."

*****

"Mate. That's 10 books. You wanna keep goin', go get my books an we can gamble till my out-date comes."

"Tay, I got the stamps, lets run it back."

"I'm through dog," I told Cee. I had punished him on the chess board five straight games. As I was leaving the table somebody yelled, and said that I had a door call. "Go get my bread," I told Cee as I passed him on my way outside. When I stepped on the porch I saw Sig standing down at the end of the walkway.

As I headed down the walk, Sig said, "What up doe, my man?"

"I can't call it. What's the tip?" I said, as we gave each other a play, and friendly embrace.

"Let's shoot up to rec. It's too nice to be in that unit."

"Aiight, let me go throw on my shoes." As I was walking back in the unit, Cee was coming out and gave me my 10 books of stamps. I went in and put my shoes on and left right back out. We stopped at H unit to see if any of the kitchen workers had any veggies, then went up to the rec yard.

It was a typical May day on the yard. The hoop courts were full, the weight pit was full, and people were standing around just kicking it. We hit the track and Sig instantly fired up a blunt. After he hit it a few times he passed it to me and said, "I gave them Atlanta niggas 5 grams over a week ago and dude who calls it for them ain't gave me shit, or even said shit."

"Did you holla at 'em?"

"Phuck yea, I holla'd at that bitch ass nigga. You know me. The nigga said he'd get at me, but that was three days ago. And wheneva I see 'im, he don't say shit. So, today I see 'im and 'bout eight more of his homies, they all just look at me. So I grim them hoe-ass niggas like, yeah, it's on."

"Well, dig," I said, "since you and Yalmo leave next year, we…"

Sig snatched the blunt from his lips and said, "Phuck that! Them hoe ass niggas owe. They thank they beastin sumin', so we butchering 'em niggas."

I looked at Sig and started laughing. He said, "What choo laughing at?"

"Nigga, calm down. All I was gon say was since you and Yahmo go home next year, we can put a hit on 'em. But since you wanna butcher the niggas, we can do it tomorrow. What unit dude in?"

"We can't do it tomorrow cause it's anotha one I wanna get."

"Aiight, hurry up and find out so we can do this."

"I am cause tomorrow is Thursday, and I wanna be able to hit they ass Saturday or Sunday when muthaphuckas don't have ta get up for work."

Over the next couple of days, Sig found out the two he really wanted were in E unit. They weren't bunkies, but their bunkies were their homies, so it worked out perfect. We were gonna be able to hit all four in one trip. Sunday morning, we went to E unit. They had a foul officer working, so that put shit on hold. But at the softball game, we saw Jonathan, the one Sig gave the work to, going into the rec room.

Ito came up in the bleachers where me and Sig were sitting. "That hoe ass nigga Jonathan just went in the gym," he said. "We got thangs up here. Yall can hit that bitch now. Ain't nobody in the gym but my homies. I'll go in there and start a game up an yall can handle ya business."

Sig got up and said, "Let's roll."

We went in the exercise room and Ito brought us two fiberglass swords and two pairs of work gloves. Jonathan was in the bathroom by his self. We threw on the gloves, ran up in there and pushed it to him. He tried to cover up and my first jab caught him in the arm. Sig was pushing and pulling like it was an exercise. I caught him once in the face, then I went to the body. After a few body shots, I broke it off in him.

While I was carefully taking my sweat suit off, I told Sig, "Come on nigga. Get up outta that shit."

We left out in gray shirts, gray shorts and gray socks. Leaving behind a pile of clothes, and Jonathan, with multiple stab wounds, two broke off plastic knives, and a weak pulse.

Ito was able to get us some shoes to throw on, so we left ours in the bathroom with the rest of that damaged shit.

Luckily, they called the ten minute move while I was tying my shoes. I was in the unit putting my clothes in the washer machine when I heard Monique yell, "Everybody to your cells. Lock down!"

When I came out of the laundry room, officers were in the unit helping to lock doors. At first, I was nervous, then I realized they were just 'aiding and assisting'. Later that night I laid on my bunk thinking about what happened, and the fact that I may have killed a man. It was bloody and gruesome and probably a horrific sight, to some, but it was nothing to me, in comparison to seeing my brother get his brains blew out.

Chapter Ten

"Baby, what's taking you so long?" Rome yelled in the bedroom to Landa.

"Here I come. Dang!"

Getting up and grabbing the car keys off the end table, Rome said, "I called from over Junior's house over an hour ago and told you to get dressed. I bet you was on the damn phone gossiping."

Landa turned around like a model, then placed her hand on her hip and asked, "Do I look like I've been on the damn phone! Or do I look like I've been gettin' ready?"

She was wearing a teal green sun dress with some matching Manolo mules. Her long hair was in two braids that hung over each shoulder and rested on the top of each breast.

Looking into her hazelnut colored eyes, Rome said, "You are looking scrumptious. I hope, I really hope, I don't have to phuck nobody up down there for making lewd comments."

"Likewise," she said, checking out her man from head to toe.

Rome was 6'1" towering over the 5'2" Landa. His dark skin meshed perfectly with her paper bag brown complexion. He was sporting some black Pelle shorts, with an orange Pelle wife beater and

some black Nike Air Force Ones. His 26" Byzantine with the iced out
R was beaming as it hung around his smooth, velvet like skin,
brazing like his Rolex watch and pinkie ring.

When they got downtown, it was almost 3 o'clock, but traffic was
still thick. People came down merely to try and find a good spot on
the River Front for the 4th of July fireworks. After Rome parked, him
and Landa got out and started walking toward Hart Plaza to enjoy
some of the holiday festivities. Standing at the African stand that sold
oils and incense, Rome saw Tay's man Quincy. "Que, what up doe?"

Turning around and seeing who was talking to him, "Que said,
Young Rome, what's happening? I ain't seen yo' lil ass since Tay's
trial. What's up wit' 'im?"

"He strait. He got two and some change left. I go see 'im all da
time."

"Next time you holla at 'im, tell 'im I said what up?'

"Fa sho'."

"It's funny that I ran into you. I thought I saw that nigga Tripp."

With an excited, but serious expression on his face, Rome said,
"You bullshitin'! Where you see that hoe ass nigga at?"

"Last week I was over this bitch crib on Tracy and Puritan, and I
thought…"

Cutting Que off, and nodding his head real fast, Rome said, "Yeah,
that was that bitch! His ole girl stay on the same block as Coles
funeral Home, and his baby mama stay next door to 'er."

"Well then, that was him"

"Good looking, Dog," Rome said, giving Que some dap. "So what
else you been into? Rome asked.

"All I been doing is phuckin' wit' them trees. I can't get no love
on the yay tip since Tay' been gone, so I'm moving lbs."

"Not ta just be in your business, but what choo getting? I got the funk all day fa da low-low."

"I usually get 'bout 50 fa nine a bow".

Shaking his head, Rome said, "Baby, give me a pen and a piece of paper." Landa handed Rome a pen and a piece of paper out of her Gucci bag. Rome wrote down his beeper and cell numbers, then gave the paper to Que. "Make sure you get at me. What I'm a give you for 700 is gon' seem unreal."

"Aiight, I'm a hit choo later on this week."

"Bet. And good looking out on that other info."

Leaving the fireworks, Rome sat in deep concentration while Landa was driving. She knew that his focus was on whoever Tripp was, and she also knew that he intended to do something to him. Why? She didn't know, but she knew not to ask questions about this side of his lifestyle.

Reaching over and grabbin his hand, she asked, "What's on your mind, Boo?"

"Nothing. I enjoyed spending the day wit' my baby. Now I can't wait to get you home and break you off."

"Hmm. I can't wait either," she said, mashing the gas.

As they sped up, Rome turned up the Black street CD and listened to them sing about money not being able to buy you love. Then he pulled out his cell phone and called Junior. When he heard Junior's voice, he said, "Main man. I'm on the Lodge. Me and Landa just left the fireworks. We going ta chill for the rest of the night, but tomorrow we got sumin' to do."

Junior said, "My cell is on 24/7, and I'll be no further than some gallons of gas away."

Chapter Eleven

"Baby, it's about time for us to get up outta this apartment. The beginning of next year we gon look fa us a crib. It's 'bout time fa us ta shoot to da burbs."

"Sounds like a plan to me, 'cause we don't even have enough room for our clothes," Landa replied.

They had just walked in from a two month trip to Jamaica. Bags were everywhere and there were a few more in the car. "I'll go get the rest of the bags and you be naked and bent over when I get back."

"Okay Daddy," Landa said, smiling.

When Rome came back in the house, he set the bags down. "Woman, where you at?" He called out as he walked into the bathroom to pee.

"In here obeying orders from my daddy," he heard her say from their bed room.

While he was washing his hands, Landa walked pass the bathroom in her rob and said, "Somebody's at the door. I'll get it. It's probably Tasha."

Rome walked into the dining room ready to tell Tasha that Landa couldn't have company. Instead, he saw two black men with detective badges hanging around their necks. Landa was standing there with a worried expression on her face. "What yall want?" Rome asked, as he looked from one cop to the other.

"Are you Jerome Harris?" One of the cops asked.

"Yeah."

"You are under arrest for the murder of Kevin Thompson."

Landa let out a low scream and fainted. The other officer caught her, and laid her on the couch. Crystal, the woman in the apartment next door, was walking pass. Handcuffed, Rome called her name. When she peeked in, he said, "Stay wit' Landa fa me. And call my sister Tasha and tell 'er I've been arrested fa murder. When Landa clears 'er head, tell 'er to call Mr. Peppers and tell 'im what happened, and ta come down ta 1300." He gave her Tasha's numbers, both the house and her cell phone.

When they were pulling off, he saw Landa come out of the building screaming and Crystal trying to hold her up.

As soon as they walked into the interrogation room and took off the cuffs, the officer identified as Burks slammed Rome, face first, onto the desk. Officer Lampkin pulled Burks off Rome and offered him a chair. When Rome sat down, Detective Lampkin offered him a cigarette. Rome told him, "I don't smoke, and yall can save that good cop-bad cop shit. When my lawyer gets here, we'll see what he wants to talk about. But til then, yall might as well get on wit' cha booking procedures." It was apparent that Rome wasn't going to talk, so both detectives left the room.

After about three hours, Mr. Peppers came into the room. Rome raised his head up off the desk, and when he saw his attorney, he said, "What's up.'

Shaking his head, he said, "you've managed to get yourself in some real shit. And, you can believe I'm not the only one who's gonna recognize that name. The feds will probably snatch this from the state, if the evidence is overwhelming enough."

"So, how we gon go at 'em?"

"Jerome, I do drug cases. Murder is out of my league. But my pal, Sam Levitchz, is the best. I've already called him. He's very expensive, but well worth every penny."

"Well, when can I bond up outta here?"

"They'll probably make you wait the full 72 hours before they charge you, which'll be Wednesday. Then, you'll be arraigned Thursday morning. And truthfully, you probably won't get a bond on this murder charge."

"So how much do I need ta give ole boy ta get started?"

"Considering this is going to be a lengthy process, if you can, I'd advise that you start with $100,000.00 and let him use whatever is necessary. If, for some reason, he gets it thrown out or something, the remaining balance can be refunded."

"Okay, I'll have my woman take it to 'im in the morning. When do you think he'll be able ta come and see me?" Rome asked, sitting now with his head in his hands.

"He'll probably be down here tomorrow or Tuesday. I'm going to come with im. Right now, I'm going to try to find out what they have. But, Jerome?"

Rome looked up into Mr. Peppers face, "Yeah?"

"Be strait up with Sam. The more truthful you are, the better he can plan your defense. And the better your chances are that those twelve jurors agree on a not guilty verdict."

*****

Rome was formally charged with first degree murder Tuesday morning, and transferred to the new side of Wayne county Jail that afternoon. Shortly after he arrived, he was called out for an attorney visit.

When he walked into the conference room ,Mr. Peppers was sitting down, and standing at the table, looking thru some papers, was a short white man. He had balding hair and glasses that sat on a long pointy nose. And, he was wearing the best suit that Sears had to offer.

"How you doing?" Rome asked, as Mr. Peppers stood to shake his hand.

"Fine. Sam, this is Jerome Harris. Jerome, Sam Levitchz," Mr. Peppers introduced the two men. They shook hands, then they all sat down. Once they were seated, Mr. Peppers passed Rome a piece of paper. "One second, gentlemen," Sam said, as he got up and left the room. Rome nodded in Sam's direction, "Okay," then began to unfold the piece of paper that Pep had given him

Written in red ink was a name and an address: *Carlton Trump, 16133 Tracy, age 14*. Rome re-folded the paper and placed it in his sock. He looked at Pep, who then kinda raised his arms and shrugged his shoulders. Rome dropped his head in his hands and started shaking his head.

"Well, Mr. Harris, your arraignment is tomorrow at 10:00 am." Mr. Levitchz said as he returned to the room. "You'll plead not guilty. Seeing that you've retained my services, I'll ask that bond be set at a reasonable amount, then the prosecution will ask that bond be denied, and their request will be granted.

From what I gather, they have no gun, no prints, or any other physical evidence. However, they have a witness that says they saw you leave out of the house of the victim and get into an awaiting car after numerous shots were fired. The victim was shot eight times, so the witness statement is accurate as far as the shots go. Now, since there's no evidence, what-so- ever, just a witness that I have to shred on the stand, I'd like to have a speedy trial and not allow the police to uncover anything, if it's there."

Looking at Mr. Levitchz, Rome said, "Pep said I have the best, so I'm a follow your plan."

Gathering his paperwork and standing up to shake Rome's hand, Sam said, "Well, that's how we'll proceed. I'll see you tomorrow morning."

*****

Rome was led into the courtroom handcuffed in the front. Once the cuffs were removed, he headed towards the defense table. As he was walking, he saw his mother, Landa and Tasha seated behind his table. After him and Mr. Levitchz had a brief exchange, Rome sat, then turned around and told them that he was alright, and to stop looking so sad. When the judge entered the court room, everyone rose, then sat down. The proceedings took no longer than 10 minutes. It went exactly like Sam said it would. Rome entered a not guilty plea, and bond was denied.

At the conclusion of the arraignment, Sam told Rome, "I'll file for a speedy trial so we can get this thing on the road. I know sitting in jail stinks, but whenever I'm defending, I like my clients' chances."

About an hour after Rome came back from court, his name was called for a visit. When he walked into the visiting booth, Landa was sitting on the stool and Tasha was standing behind her waving. Divided by the glass wall between them, waving back, he sat down and picked up the telephone receiver that hung on the wall. "Where's my mama at?"

"Downstairs, waiting for us. She said she'll see you in court and when you come home, but not behind this glass," Landa answered, touching the glass and starting to cry.

"Baby, stop crying. This shit will be over sooner than you think. And we'll be house shopping and planning our wedding. Okay?"

Landa was crying too hard to verbally answer. She just shook her head. Then, in a barely audible voice, she said, "Hold on, Tasha wants to talk to you."

"Take care of my baby," Rome said to Tasha as soon as she placed the telephone to her ear.

"You know I got 'er. She'll be aiight. This is the hardest part."

"I know. So, what's up wit' choo?"

"I talked to Tay yesterday. He said for you to stay strong and Pep knows what to look for in situations like this. He said he'll call him to let him know that the same rules apply for you too."

"Tell Tay he already got that info for me, but I don't like it."

"Okay. And, he said expenses are nothing. Whateva your lawyers need, he gets. Just let us know."

"Aiight, I appreciate that, but I believe I'll be straight. But, what I do need, is for you ta get wit' my lil' mans Tee. Tell 'im ta come see me a-sap. His numbers are in my phone at home. And, thanx Tasha."

"No problem. Take care. Here you go, "she said to Landa, as she passed her the receiver.

Chapter Twelve

"So, what's the latest haps wit' Rome's case?" I asked Tash while we were visiting.

"Ain't nothin' changed. Except the judge said he won't grant another continuance for the prosecution. He's given them two, but said witness or no witness the trial will start May 8th, or they can dismiss the charges."

"What are they sayin' 'bout the witness?"

"The prosecution insinuated that since Rome killed the man that told on his cousin, that' he'll surely kill someone that's going to tell on him. The judge told the PA if they don't have any proof to support those allegations, not to mention it in his court room again."

I looked at Tash and just shook my head. Then, she asked me, "Do you think Rome would have a child killed?"

"I don't think he would, but I know he don't wanna do all day in the joint either. A muthaphucka will do whateva ta stay outta here."

Tash leaned her head on my shoulder and said, "I'm glad you don't have that much longer. I miss you so much! Plus, I hate you being here with that bitch that's always smilin' in my face and likes playin' games wit' my baby."

*****

I was in my cell during 4:00 p.m. count, by myself doing a lot of thinking. Yahmo went home yesterday, and Sig leaves in about 90 days, on the 18th of August. All I have to do is walk down these last 27 months and it'll be on again.

A lot of questions have been answered during the course of this bit. First off, I never doubted Tashs' love for me, but I did have my doubts about her riding it out from the beginning to the end. There were a few times when shit was shaky as hell, but we overcame all of that. She's handled my business affairs like a true champ. Too bad she thinks that my properties and land are gonna keep me out of the game. I must admit that I was surprised that I felt nothing when me and Sig put in that work. I had been the cause of one's mortal state before, but never in such a hands on manner. Knife play is much different than gun play. It takes a certain kind of individual to indulge in a life ending encounter like that. And I'm one of them.

Rome has turned out to be a real surprise too. He buckled down and became a real hustler. I do hate that school became secondary, momentarily, then all together out of the question, but who could blame him. The boy started making some real money. However, the real shocker was when he did that rat ass nigga Tripp. I always figured Rome for the type that would pay somebody rather than get his own hands dirty. Although the jury came back with a not guilty verdict, I still know cuz took care of his business. Then turned around and sealed his own fate by making a move that the average man couldn't and wouldn't have made. We haven't talked about it, and probably never will. At least I'll never bring it up, 'cause I know that that was the hardest decision he's ever had to make.

*****

"Where does your brother get that weed?" I asked Monique.

"I don't know. I just get some of it from him to bring to you. Why? It's good?"

"Hell naw. It's fair, but for him to be in the streets like you say, he ain't plugged."

Since Yahmo and Sig were gone home, and I only had about 10 months left, I had stopped hustling and had Monique bring me some weed every now and then, to smoke. I couldn't smoke like I wanted to cause for some reason they were pissing me like crazy, and it was too late in the game for me to be catching dirty urines.

"I told you that he ain't a Kingpin, but he's big time in our lil' city."

"Don't worry 'bout it. Next time I'll have my cousin shoot you some. I ain't 'bout ta be gettin' my system dirty and not be high as hell."

She gave me a **whatever** look, then said, "Do you ever think about what's goin' to happen wit' you and Tasha when you get home?"

"I already know what's gon happen. I told you not to worry 'bout it. Me and you are gon be aiight. From what choo tell me there's a lot of business opportunities down this way. I'm a keep you busy."

"What choo mean?" She asked.

"I mean I'm a get choo some shit of you own, 'cause you're quitting this job. I ain't 'bout ta have you 'round all these niggas everyday."

She looked at me and started batting her eyes. Then she asked me, "What, you don't trust me? Or are you insecure?"

I started shaking my head and waving my hands and told her, "It ain't got shit to do wit' me trusting you, or being insecure. It's about me being smart enough to keep you from gettin' into any compromising positions. A man's prison would be a helluva spot to test the Virgin Mary, so I definitely ain't gon leave you 'round these vultures."

Monique busted out laughing. "Even though you wouldn't have shit to worry about, I feel you. Since I quit going to beauty school when I got this job I guess now would be a good time to go back, huh?"

"Yup. I told you a long time ago that I'd take care of you, and I meant that. Start applying to da school you're going to. And take some business courses too."

"Is that what choo had Tasha do?"

"Mo, don't start no shit!"

"What? I just asked a simple question."

"Your simple ass know what I'm talking 'bout. The stuff I'm telling you to do is not only for me. In fact it's more beneficial to you."

"I know. I was just playing, dang. Why you get mad?"

"Cause I don't want choo thinking that I have you do what I have 'er do. That kind of thinking can cause you to lose focus of what's real."

"And what's real?"

"My feelings for you. Don't think that I don't care about you, and that you're not important to me. Okay?"

"All right."

*****

69

During the home run stretch I laid all the way back. I never did get into the weight lifting, but I had to be toned up, so I ran a lot, did push-ups and worked the shit out of my abs. If I wasn't working out I wasn't seen. When I got six months to the door I made Monique quit and start coming to this bitch as a visitor, instead of an employee.

At first she said that it was awkward, but I quickly erased those feelings. She learned to not care about what others thought, and to focus on us. I was the only person whose thoughts should matter, I told her. And of course I was right.

Besides going on visits and working out, reading was my only recreation. I constantly kept my nose in the 48 Laws of Power, The Art of War and Machevelli The Prince. Running Detroit's underworld was my goal, and those three books were the treadmills I used to exercise my mind. A living hell was coming to an end, but everyday forth would be like heaven on earth.

When Your Associates R More Dangerous Than U

Part 2

Murder City Niggas

...Phuck it buy the coke cook the coke cut it
Know the bitch fore ya call yourself lovin' it
Nigga in a Benz fuckin' it...
Notorious B.I.G.

Chapter Thirteen

It was my first day back on the streets, and as B.I.G. said, 'Thangs Done Changed'. When I left Pelle' Pelle' and Coogi were some of the more above average clothing lines that we were rocking. Now I couldn't even pronounce the name of the shit they were wearing. Luckily my family ensured that I at least look like I know what's going on.

Rome came and picked me up from the halfway house to take me to mine. He figured that we'd be able to kick it for a hot second before I go get engulfed in the pussy.

When I stepped out of the halfway house I was donned in a pair of black Sean John jeans, a cream Sean John sweater and some black Timberland boots. Rome jumped out of his 2000 Cadillac Escalade with a big smile on his face.

As we embraced he said, "Damn Bra, welcome home. I didn't think this day was gon' ever get here."

"Yeah, I had a few minor setbacks at the end. Dudes tend to test ya resolve when your time comes, and theirs is still out of reach, yunno." Rome stood looking at me for a couple of seconds. "It's me," I told him.

"Naw. I'm just checking out your attire. The gear is cool, but that leather gots ta go. Throw this on," he said, opening up the back door of his truck. He retrieved what appeared to be a coat, covered in white plastic.

"Nigga it's November! You know what we wear when it's cold, and we can afford to wear it."

"My man," I said with a smile, and proceeded to take off the leather. It was time to put on the waist length mink, with the hood that Rome was pulling from under the plastic. Once I put the mink on, and received the nod of approval, we jumped in the truck and struck out.

"I see you've recovered from the murder trial and got back on track," I said, rubbing the wood that seemed to decorate the entire interior of his truck.

"Ain't no question. The only thing that's prevented me from gettin' money was dem' bars."

I started waving my finger and shaking my head grinning, "Not so fast my friend. Dem' bars ain't stop me."

"Okay, you got me. But what's on the agenda now that you don't have those kinda restraints? After five and some change I know you got a lot of plans."

"We ain't got enough time ta talk about all of my plans and ideas. Just know that its 'bout ta be me and you baby. I should only be in that center 'bout 90 days. During that time I can kinda get a feel for the pulse of 'The City'.

We rode in silence, and I took in the surroundings that had only been a memory a couple of days ago. "As long as shit on your end and my end is tight, we're gon' flourish. When I say our Ends, I mean the crews that we assemble.

"Rome," he briefly looked at me, "dudes gotta be strong. If we get word, and we verify it, that they're leaking we gotta eliminate 'em. Fa real!"

The conversation came to a halt when we pulled up to the house. I must say the new house Tash got while I was gone was nice looking. I jumped out of the truck and gave Rome a play. Then I told him, "I love you dog. Be careful."

He looked at me with a weary look, and said, "I love you too."

I just smiled and shut the door, and then I headed into my domain.

*****

Tash opened the door in a red silk robe and greeted me with a warm hug, and kissed me with such emotion and sensuality that it seemed like she'd been practicing for this day since the day I left.

The house smelled like Steve's Soul Food. I looked around the house at the lavish furnishings with pride. Tash led me to the living room, and told me, "Sit here on the couch for one minute." She disappeared into the kitchen, and I could hear plates and other utensils being moved around.

Just as I was about to open my mouth to speak, Tash said, "Come here."

I stopped in the doorway. The table was beautifully set, but I was unaware of its contents because Tash stood at the other end naked. With one hand on the back of the chair and the other arm out to the side, standing in a welcoming pose, she said, "Welcome home Daddy."

I instantly started to undress, but kept my eyes glued on her, still firm, 32 C size titties, golden thighs and, meant for Guess, hips. "I think I'll skip dinner. Dessert looks more nutritious."

In a husky voice, Tash said, "Well, what you waiting on? Come and get it."

I went and pulled her into my arms and pulled her head back by her hair, and started biting and kissing on her neck. I licked from her neck to her cleavage and sucked on her left titty, before scooping her up and sitting her on the table. She laid back, and I traced my tongue from each breast down to her navel. I stopped there and licked around, and inside it before I traveled further south. After giving the midway lips a few light kisses, I was about to tend to the inner thighs, but Tash raised up, breathing hard, and said, "Tay," I looked up at her, "stop playing and fuck me!"

When I entered her and began stroking, she put her arms back and palms down to support her weight then flung her head back. I pulled her closer to the end of the table, and when I put all of me inside of her, she brought her arms around and held my head in both hands and just looked at me. She looked down then back at me and said, "That's it Daddy!" Then she said, "Let me taste me," and we kissed and came to a climatic finish.

After finishing my third pork chop, I told Tash, "Now that the first one is out da way I'm really ready to get it on, before its time fa me to go back."

"You ain't said shit. Meet me up stairs. Plus I need to show you what you do at the halfway point," she said, giving me a seductive look, leaving out of the kitchen.

*****

Looking out the window as we rode back to the halfway house, I asked Tash, "Where my lil mans at?"

"He stayed wit' his Papa last night."

"I guess they got high as hell last night. Your old man believes in gettin' right. That's why I'm a have ta stay away from him. I only been out a month. I can't be droppin' no dirties. And I be wantin' ta smoke," I told Tash, as we headed to her parents house to pick up Tay, before dropping me off at the center.

Chapter Fourteen

Rome was on his way to Kentucky Fried Chicken when he saw
Trina walking into the beauty supply store on Seven Mile and
Marlowe. He hit his born and when she looked up and saw Rome, she
waved for him to come to her. Rome busted a right onto Marlowe,
then a quick right into the store alley and whipped into the parking lot.

"What's up girl?" He asked when he let the window down.

"You. I just wanted to let choo know that Tone will be home next
Tuesday. Next weekend I'm a have a dinner at the house."

"Aiight. I know you're glad. Santa comin' ta see you early this
year. Anything you want us ta bring?"

"Naw. Just let Tasha know, so her and Tay can come."

Grabbing his cell phone to return a page he'd just gotten, Rome
said, "Aiight. I'll holla at choo later."

Once he finished his call, he shot to KFC and went to pick up
Junior. While they were riding to the eastside, Rome filled Junior in
on why he was in such a euphoric state. "Dog, Jorge just hit me and

says he done shot me a Christmas present. He wants me to come out there after the holidays."

"Fa what?"

"I haven't the slightest idea, but I'm sure it's about business. Which is good, 'cause I ain't gettin' no mo' yay 'til we can get it for the low- low, yunno?"

Smoking on a blunt, Junior looked over at Rome and said, "Makes sense to me. Plus, the trees not only pay the bills, they pay for the wants as well. But I ain't gon' lie, ain't no money like cocaine money…"

Then they looked at each other and threw their heads back, and in a singing voice, sang "Except heroine money!" They laughed and gave each other some dap.

"But on da real, I bet Tay is gon' wanna dabble in that field as well. He been spending quality time wit' his family, so we haven't really kicked it on the business tip. But Tay seems different. I can't really put my finger on it, but…"

The look on Junior's face became serious as he looked over at Rome. "Road Dog, when you do a bit, and you one of dem 'bout your paper kinda niggas' shit is different. You've had years ta sit back and put shit together in your mind, but there's a gate that prevents you from doin' it. So, when you get out, a lack of focus is the only thing that can prevent you from doin' it. And if you serious 'bout gettin' it, it'll show.

Rome just nodded his head as an understand-it gesture, but remained silent.

Then Junior asked 'im, "Where we headed?"

"Ta pick up my Christmas present."

Chapter Fifteen

I was sitting around the house smoking me a joint. I figured that since I didn't smoke none while I was in the halfway house, that it wouldn't take much to get me high.

Every since me and Sig talked last month at Trina and Tone's house, I'd been trying to put something together. Sig's main man had gotten killed and the people that I was phuckin' with, before I got knocked, was filling up beds in the BOP. Rome was getting a few hundred pounds, but weed money was play money, and I ain't come home to play.

I was in deep meditation, listening to Beans speak 'The Truth', when the doorbell rang.

"What up doe, my man?" I said when I opened the door.

Giving me a play, Sig said, "Ain't shit poppin, just shooting thru ta see what choo getting' into."

I shut the door and we went into the living room and Sig sat down. After I turned the music down, I went into the kitchen, grabbed two Coronas and came back. I gave Sig one and sat back in the recliner.

"Slow motion this way. Figure I'm a hit one of my mans and see what's poppin'. It's like these lames out here afraid ta plug us in. And we comin' wit' money."

Sig shrugged his shoulders and took a sip of his beer. "You know how it go. Dudes either ain't got the work to fill the order, or they the middle man and put they tax on it. I'm still enjoying being free and ain't pressed, 'cause a dog is gon' eat once the hunger strikes."

I wasn't starving, but I had real plans that I was ready to put into effect. After I asked Rome what was up with the Mexican? And he told me he only phucks with trees, I hit Yahmo. He told me he'd been expecting to hear from me, and to fly out so we could talk.

*****

Yahmo had a big ass beach front house off the coast. It had seven bedrooms, all equipped with Jacuzzis in the bathrooms. With the exception of the library, which had that sink-six inches-when-you step-on-it carpet, every floor was done in some form of marble. I must say that I was highly impressed with his crib. We sat out on the patio smoking a blunt after he gave me the grand tour. I extended my compliments and got right to business.

"You know I need good prices and bomb work. I'm sure I can put together enough change to…"

He stuck his hands out, motioning me to 'stop'. "Whoa Tay. I was serious when I said we gon' get money out here on these streets. Man, we done a bit together, hustled in the belly of the beast together and done kicked it about everything from past happenings to future plans. I know you was out here doin' your thang before you got knocked. What money you already got is yours to keep. And not to insult you, but, it's nothin'."

I surely wasn't insulted, or offended, cause I knew he wasn't trying to belittle me, by any means. He was merely stating the obvious. His living arrangements could attest to the difference in our financial status.

"Tay, if you ready, and I assume you are, or you wouldn't have hit me; in two weeks I'll have 500 birds fly your way. Guaranteed delivery and pick up every month from then until the earth stops spinning."

My face didn't display the elation that I felt inside, but the smile couldn't be helped. I reached across the table and shook Yahmo's hand.

"My only question to you is what's my ticket?"

He smiled, and in a voice like Tony Montana, said, "On drop off and pick up day, I'll have 500 for you, and you have 4.5 for me."

*****

It was two weeks before the 2002 Super bowl, and one week before the first shipment. I was in a royal blue Taurus rental, talking to Rome as we headed to my house to meet Sig.

"It's finally on," I said. "I hope you got your team together. Next Tuesday we'll be right. And off the muscle you got a 100 comin'."

"A hundred birds?" Rome asked. With a look of disbelief. "Yeah nigga! Is that too much?"

Rome shook his head and said, "Naw. I knew you were puttin' sumin' together, but I'm a be real wit' choo, I figured that since your people had gotten knocked, that we was gon' go in together ta get 20 or sumin'. I had no idea that shit was gon' be this gravy this fast."

"Truthfully, I didn't either," I said. "But, I'm not overwhelmed by it. The plug came sooner than later, and I'm ready ta do this. An like

I was saying, you got 100 comin' every month. All you gotta give me is a mil."

As I pulled into the driveway, Sig got out of his car. "Yall must got somethin' planned, calling me away from this cold lil hoe that I just met."

"Nigga, I got hoes!" I said, getting out of the car and heading to my house.

"Oh yeah?"

"Yeah." I answered, as I opened up the front door.

Once inside, I grabbed a few beers and Sig put a twist to the buds. I rubbed my hands together with a smirk on my face an' asked him, "Is the dog hungry?"

"As a hostage!"

"Well if you like birdies I'll have 100 for ya Tuesday."

"Sig jumped up off the couch and gave me a play. He stepped back, looked at me, and said, "Nigga, you been 'bout your business. I taught you well grasshopper."

We were all so happy that we was on our way to doing what we wanna do, that we all just busted out laughing.

Being affiliated with a line that's distributing 100 keys was nothing new to Sig. I had been the holder of 100 or so myself, so moving the work wasn't going to be a problem. And Rome's maturity in the game was evident. He just never had an opportunity like this one, so I was as comfortable mashing that shit on him as I was with Sig. However, by me having just left the Feds, and seeing, first hand, how they're trapping dudes, I had some safety provisions that I needed to discuss with them.

"Dig," I said, looking at Sig, then Rome. "We gon' do this on a higher level. We all got muthaphuckas that we phuck wit'. Assemble your crews, but it'd be best to have one man handle the distribution to them. And him, and him only come holla at choo."

"So, in other words, us three only meet amongst each other?" Rome asked.

"Exactly. 'Cause what I'ma do is have Pep put P.I.'s on our crew leaders," I said. "Not only can we afford it, we gon' pay 'em well. That way, taking another job won't cross their minds."

"So when the heat comes down on them, we know it's not far from us." I nodded my head, yeah. "And that'll at least give us a heads up," Sig continued.

"Yep." I said, "And since we'll have work all day long, of course we gon' put shit down here, but we also gon' send niggas ta Flint, Saginaw, the Creek and all the other small spots in Michigan. Wherever there's money ta be made, we'll send representatives, and we'll be da ones getting' it."

"Can the lawyer be trusted?" Sig asked.

"Without a doubt. And he's gon' make sure we stay well informed." Rome added.

I told Sig, "As soon as you can, put some money in his pocket for a retainer. An as soon as you know who your crew leaders are, let me know. I'll pay the investigators for "Murder City Niggas'."

The weed had really taken effect, cause Sig fell out laughing, "That's what we are?"

Laughing equally as hard, I said, "Yeah, cause we gon' have ta lay it down like that in order fa niggas to heed the messages that we're 'bout ta send."

"Boy, you have really thought this out. And I'm wit' choo til the casket drops," Sig said, clutching his stomach laughing. He stood up and gave me and a play, then a manly embrace. Walking toward the door, he stopped and turned around, "What's da ticket?"

"A mil, " I said, and winked at him.

"My muthaphuckin' man! I'll holla at choo "Murder City Niggas' tomorrow."

"Well Bra, we only got a few more days to play before play time is over. What choo wanna get into?"

"I'ma stay out the way. Plus, there's some other loose ends that I need ta tie up. An I bet you do too," I told Rome.

"Like what?" He asked.

"How many houses you got pumpin' right now?"

"None. You know I only been phuckin' wit' the trees, but I still got spots. I just gotta get 'em ready."

"You know what that's called?" Looking him in the eyes, "Loose ends. By the time Tuesday comes the only thing the house should be missing is rocks. You also need residential houses not far from the spots. The last thing you wanna be doing is picking up money on Fenkell and Livernois, and riding wit' it across town."

Rome looked at me with understanding eyes and said, "Message received." He got up and put on his coat to leave. When he opened the door, he turned around and said, "Right now I'm goin' home ta spend the evening wit' my lovely woman. And tomorrow, I'll wake up in the morning and start tying shit up."

I nodded my approval and told him "I love you, and be careful."

"Aiight. Love you too."

Chapter Sixteen

"Girl, I'm so sick of counting this shit that I don't know what to do," Tasha told Landa, as she threw another $100,000.00 stack into the box. "I only have to do it once a month, but this shit is a headache. And it stinks."

Putting money into the money machine, Tasha looked at Landa and said, "I got so much shit, that before my birthday, I told Tay all I wanted was to spend an eventful day with my Tays, and the night wit' the oldest one."

Lightheartedly, Landa laughed. "The first time I had to count a large sum of money it was fun. But it did get old, quick. And it's nowhere near this much," she said, glancing at the three already full boxes, and the other knotted rolls and bags of money in the room.

"Aside from your accounting gig, how's real estate school?" Landa asked. "Actually it's quite interesting. When I was accepted to Columbia Law School, I had to put it off 'cause my Tays' needed me most. But I didn't think I'd enjoy this real estate shit so much. Tay wanted to constantly buy stuff, so it's actually what I needed to do. Plus, it's not only about houses and apartment buildings. Getting land and developing it is where the money is. All it requires is the finances and ones vision." Waving her hand around, she said, "And it's obvious we ain't lacking in the finance department," and pointing to her head, she continued, "and this is full of visions."

"Well, I'm glad that I'll have a real estate agent that I can trust, 'cause I start Culinary Arts School next month, and I got a feeling Rome is going to be buying a lot of property as well."

"You know I got choo."

"You know, it's really a trip that tonight is the first time that we're all going out together. Me and Rome been together for four years, and I know he's been looking forward to a night like this, for four years."

Grabbing her keys and purse, Landa told Tasha, "I'm on my way to get my hair done. I'll see yall later on tonight at the club."

"Okay girl, I'll holla."

Tasha checked the clock and saw that it was 9:36 a.m. She'd been up since 7:00 a.m. counting money and still had a ways to go. 'Whatever woman thought that a Hustler's better half didn't do nothing but live good, either didn't know about the work that comes with it, because they man works, or don't know cause they man is grinding and ain't getting money,' she thought as she put another stack in the machine.

By the time Tasha got everything together and got out of the shower, it was a quarter to two, and her hair appointment was at 2:30. After she got dressed, she called Tay on his cell and told him to pick up Lil Tay from school 'cause she'd be in the salon forever, then she left.

As soon as she walked in the shop, Jason came switching toward her, grabbed her hand, then led her to the back room. Closing the door behind them, he said, "Gurll, let me tell you! That fine muthaphucka came in here looking for you."

"Who?"

"I don't know his name," he said, smacking his lips and batting his eyes.

"The bald, fine muthaphucka you used ta go out wit'."

She instantly knew who he was talking about. Her mouth dropped. "Uh huh, that's him. He said he hadn't heard from you, so he went by your house, and I got nervous until he said you'd moved.

"Anyway, when I wouldn't tell him when your next appointment was, he gave me this number," he handed her a piece of paper, "and told me to tell you to call him." Tasha just stood speechless. "I take it that he doesn't know about Mr. Tay?" Tasha shook her head, no. "Well, good luck, " he said. "I hate to be the bearer of bad news. If it is bad news? Now, come on so I can fix that mess on your head."

It was a few minutes pass six when Tasha left the salon. By the time she pulled into Rome and Landa's driveway it was 6:37. As soon as Landa opened the door, Tasha whispered, "Is Rome here?"

"Naw. I just talked to him. He's at your house. Why? What's up?

"Bitch! That muthaphucka Alex done popped up at the shop and gave Jason his number to give to me. He wants' me to call him."

"No the phuck he didn't!"

"Yes the phuck he did! 'Said he came by the house, but I moved."

"When's the last time you talked to 'im?

"The last time I seen him was when we went over to Canada and stayed at Wheels Inn for the weekend. That was in the summer of 2000. I dodged him for, like, two weeks while I was moving. Then, I called him one day when I was on the highway going to see Tay, and told him I was on my way to Law School, and I'd call him when I get there and give him all my information. He started asking a lot of questions, but I told him we'd talk when I pull over and get a room. Until today, I hadn't heard nothing from 'im."

"Tasha, this ain't good. If Tay finds out, muthaphuckas gonna get hurt! And not only Alex.

"I know. I'll just call and tell…"

Landa threw her hands up in the air, shaking her head and looked at Tasha, and said, "You love playin wit' fire, don't choo? Leave that man alone! You don't owe him no explanation. Yall had what choo had, and it was fun while it lasted. But it's over and been over for a over a year."

"You're right. I ain't gon' call 'im. I'm 'bout to go home an I'll see you later."

During her ride home Tasha thought about Alex. She knew that Landa was right, but for some reason, feelings that she had suppressed to the point that she'd forgotten, or that she didn't even realize she had for him, began to rise.

*****

Tasha and Tay pulled up to club Platinum on Six Mile. As usual, there was an array of ballers and their lady friends. Ice was blingin' and the latest fashions were on display. When they stepped out of the 2002 steel gray Cadillac Sedan Deville, it was apparent that a Don and his dame had arrived. Cats greeted Tay with the utmost respect. Some asked when they could hook up, but Tay made it clear that his night out was recreational only.

Inside, they were led to the V.I.P. section by one of MCN's young soldiers. Rome and Sig greeted Tay with warm brotherly hugs. It was the first time that Tasha had seen Tay as being a real boss. He'd always been charismatic, but now his power exuded him.

Tasha sat down and sipped on the glass of Remy Red that Tay poured for her. "Girl, as soon as you get a chance, look over toward the bar, and please keep your facial expression the same," Landa told her.

Maintaining the same expression became difficult when, at a table by the bar, sat Alex and three other men. As if someone told him that she was looking at them, Alex raised his head and their eyes met. He gave her a wink, then resumed the conversation that he was having with his associates.

Tay was singing Usher's *You Got It Bad* in Tasha's ear as they sat cuddled up on the couch when the waitress approached the V.I.P table with two fifths of Louis XIII and two fifths' of Cristal. "Compliments of the gentlemen over there," she said to Tay, pointing to a table by the bar.

Tay sent his lieutenant, Que, to thank him personally, and extract this man's motive for his actions.

"He looks familiar as hell," Rome said, as eyes, except Tasha', were looking towards the table.

When Que came back and sat down, everyone's attention shifted to him. "He said it's nice to finally be able to put a face with the name he's been hearing. He said the gesture was purely out of respect, and if any offense was taken, he apologizes."

Tay lifted his glass toward the men by the bar. Tasha became very upset, and began to feel uneasy. Trina looked at Landa and they both stood up. "We'll be back. It's restroom time," Landa said.

"Yeah. Remy is running through me too," Tasha said, as she followed Landa and Trina to the ladies room.

"Can you believe this shit!" Tasha said when they got in the restroom. "I don't hear from him in over a year, and now he's tracking me down. And I see 'im tonight!"

"You might just need to tell Tay that you went out wit' him and get it over wit'. He'll be pissed, but he ain't gon' leave you. Hell, he was gone for damn near six years, and you held him down," Landa told her.

Trina looked at Landa and said, "Naw! He ain't gon' leave 'er," and looking at Tasha she continued, "but it's gonna be some shit behind that drink stunt. You know how men and their pride is."

With her hands on her hips, Landa asked Trina, "Well, what she gon do then?"

"Look," Tasha said, "I'm a have to call him and just let him know that I did get caught up in the moment while Tay was gone, but he's home now, and, ain't shit happening anymore." Landa had a weary look on her face. "I know you think I shouldn't call," Tasha continued, "but I can't allow him to be disrespecting Tay and Tay not even know the deal. That, more than anything else, will have him pissed off if he just happens to find out."

"You right," Landa said, in a surrendering voice. "Lets get back out there," she said, heading to the door.

Chapter Seventeen

"It's your call, my friend. Find out what it is that he wants. Terrance, you must remember that he's been a loyal associate thus far. The only headache is that he calls quite often, even though he is aware that you two have an arrangement. Deviating from the system can be hazardous, but at the same time, you don't wanna slow down that kind of progress, my friend," Javier said in a heavily accented voice.

"That is very true, and that is my reason for having to meet wit' choo in person. It's apparent that his distribution skills are remarkable, but I knew that you would want to do some investigating."

Javier nodded his head in appreciation. "Terrance, I value your business savvy. When you first entered into the initial arrangement with your partners, I was skeptical, but I've had success from dealing with men up there. And, you showed a lot of trust in wanting to allot him that much, being it was the first time you dealt with him on a business level. But, since I trust you and your judgment, I okay'd it, but still had him and the men he's most seen with checked out. Then, when he called, twice before the meeting dates, my curiosity was piqued. My first job was to make sure that he hadn't gotten into trouble and was trying to get out of it. I also wanted to see if you had something special."

"Oh, he ain't no rat. You know I wouldn't be phuckin' wit' no rats," Yahmo said, with his mouth twisted into a frown.

"Terrance, one can never be too sure. Being paranoid had kept me alive and free. Background checks allow me to get a feeling of the individuals that are somehow a part of this line. In checking out Mr. Manning, I discovered that for one, he's very smart, organized, and knows and understands this lifestyle very well. Therefore, his request surprised me none. I will not say whether you should or should not increase his shipments, but I am okay with it."

"Well, if you're in compliance, then it's a done deal." Yahmo told his associate.

After Javier left, Yahmo called Tay an asked him if he'd be interested in coming out to the coast for dinner.

Chapter Eighteen

One thing about Detroit is that it's full of hustlers, and a real money getter can move 500 keys a month, easily. So the three I had left, after I hit Rome and Sig were going fast. Along with Que, I had a few other cats that I dealt with in the past that stayed hollering at me. Aside from them, I never dealt with anyone directly. Que made sure the daily operations were moving properly. My weight houses were like heaven to young dudes that hug the block. Not only was the work the bomb! They were able to get it hard, and still get 126 grams a eighth for $1,500.00. If they wanted a key, they just got eight eighths. And what made it even better was that it was always on.

After about six months, we began to expand. The first spot that I hit was Muskegon. There were already quite a few dudes up there from home, so setting up was easy. We tend to get along and stick together when we're outside the city limits. I went up there, and once discovering who was really getting the money, I introduced myself to him as Frank. It was a cat named Dre from the Brewster projects at home. He was up there doing alright. I was up there with that fire that Rome was getting and that's how we met. We got to be alright and began to kick it more frequently.

One day he called me for some weed and I told him to come through. I was staying at a lil motel downtown. When he got there I fired up a blunt and put my play in motion. "I know you don't be selling these," I said, as I hoisted the blunt into the air.

"Naw. I like to smoke. I'd like to grab some L-bows of this shit."

"Dog, I can get you pounds of this, and birds of A-1 so you can lay it down."

"Straight up?"

"Hell yeah. I ain't up here to pedal a ounce or two of this shit."

"Well, say that then. If the work is laying like that, I'll grab 2 or 3 of 'em. If the price is right."

"How 'bout I shoot you 10 of 'em up here at 15 a piece to start wit'?

"That'll most definitely work."

"Aiight then. Next week my mans a be up here and you'll be tight."

I left that same day. When I got back, I hollered at Que and let him know what was what. That following week he assembled a team and took them up there. Every since, I've had that spot.

When Sig started sending people to Flint and Kalamazoo, and Rome ventured up to Battle Creek and Saginaw, their 100 started to seem like a little package. And I was needing more myself, 'cause I had started phuckin' around in Grand Rapids too. Yahmo came through for me a couple of times, but made it clear that we had to stick to the script from that point on. And when I told him I needed more, he told me he'd have to get back wit' me.

Things were moving at a rapid pace, I thought, as I got ready to fly out to the coast. We had accomplished a helluva lot over the past 18 months, but that call from Yahmo was a sign of better things to come.

*****

When I got back from Cali, I called Rome and Sig and told them to come through. It was always better for me to discuss business when Tash wasn't at home. I knew she'd be gone for a few hours, 'cause when I called her, after I got back, she and her Mom were out shopping.

While I waited on Rome and Sig, I went out on the patio, fired up a blunt and made a long overdue call. "What's up Baby?" I said, when she answered the phone.

"Apparently not me. I ain't heard from you in damn near two weeks. And it's been over a month since the last time I've seen you."

"Mo, don't start. Here it is, I've been fienin' to hear from you, and as soon as you hear my voice, you catch a attitude. For one, I been outta town. And, truthfully, the niggas in the streets see and hear from me more than you, Lil Tay, and anybody else."

I could hear Monique suck her teeth before she said, "I know. But I worry 'bout choo and miss you almost as much. When am I gon' see you?"

"I'll be down there next month. I'm taking Lil Tay on a Disney cruise for the 4th of July. When I get back I'll be on my way."

"You promise?"

"I promise Baby. What's up wit' the buildings? Have you found at least one?"

"I've been looking, but none of the abandoned buildings are what you want. But, I know some places where the owners might be willing to sell, if the money is right. We'll go see them when you get here.

"I did find a spot on the out skirts that would be perfect for that other shit you was talking about."

"Aiight. I appreciate you taking care of that. My brother is at the door, so I'll call you later on tonight."

"Okay. Be careful, and I love you."

"Reciprocated."

With a light chuckle, she said, "You just refuse to say it." When I didn't respond, and just gave a little chuckle of my own, she said, "Bye Boo."

Me and Rome were in the backyard and I was in the pool swimming with my old family red nose pit bull, Tara, when I heard Sig's big mouth.

"You be exercising that bitch like she's an athlete."

"This my baby and she's the mother to those beast you don't mind puttin' yo money on. What up doe?"

"I can't call it. Rome, what's da deal, baby?"

"You got the best hand. I'm just laying back trying to stay out the way."

"Well since yall both here, dig this, thangs are righteous again. So look to do whatever you want too. Next month I'm goin' to Ohio for a couple of weeks, I want one of yall to roll wit' me." I said, looking from one to the other.

"Well I know it ain't a life or death situation, 'cause you want one of us to go," Rome said, "and didn't say you need us to go wit' choo."

"Naw, it ain't nothin' real serious. I'm 'bout ta look into buying a slaughterhouse and try to get two buildings fa Mo."

With his face wrinkled up, Rome asked me "What choo getting a slaughterhouse for?"

"For one, its good legal money in it. Two, it'll be my way to get work shipped there straight from the coast. There's more risk involved if I try ta move it from here ta there.

"I don't understand," Sig said, with a questioning look on his face.

"My man told me that he can ship the birds in cows."

"Cows?" Rome asked. "Are you serious?"

"Yeah. I'm dead serious. Dude said he can put between 10 and 15 slabs in each cow. He said when they come they'll have rings on their tongues and you just pull the ring and you get 'em out through the mouth."

Sig sat up straight in his chair and said, "Damn! That's cold as hell! Muthaphuckas be coming up wit' ways to move that work. I can't wait to see this."

I sat there nodding my head, then I hunched my shoulders and said, "We're definitely being blessed. And, we gon' take full advantage of it too." I turned and looked at Rome, "I take it that you don't wanna go down that way?"

"Not if it's not just necessary. Landa's five months pregnant and I don't wanna be away from her for weeks at a time."

"Stay here, in-love-ass-nigga." We all started laughing. "I'll shot down there wit' choo," Sig continued. "It'll be nice ta go fuck some Buckeye bitches."

Chapter Nineteen

Monique and another woman were sitting on the porch when me and Sig pulled into her driveway.

"Damn, who is that on the porch wit' Mo?" Sig asked.

"I don't know. I ain't neva met her. Let's see." I said, opening the car door. Monique came and met me on the walkway. "C'mere you", I told her, with my arms outstretched.

"Damn, I've missed you," she told me, after a nice long hug and kiss.

"What's up Sig?" She said as we stepped onto the porch. "I take it that you've already introduced yourself to my cousin?"

"I'm aiight, and bet I have introduced myself."

"Baby, this is my cousin Karmel, from Phoenix. K, this is my Boo, Tay."

"Nice to meet you," I said, as we shook hands and she nodded.

Mo looked at me, "You hungry? I still got some que left over."

"I can definitely stand to break off a few ribs."

We all sat in the kitchen talking. Me and Sig punished the ribs and macaroni-cheese, while they sat there eating ice cream. As it turned out, Karmel knew a lil something about dogs, so we all clicked.

Especially her and Sig, and not just because of the dogs either. Her father had a pit farm, and had been heavy in the dog game for over 40 years, so the conversation was interesting to everybody, but Mo.

Since the sun had gone down, once we finished eating we retreated outside to sip our brews and continue talking. About 15 minutes later, a white 82 Monte Carlo pulled into the driveway behind my 2001 Dodge Intrepid. Sig and Karmel were sitting in the chairs on the porch. I was sitting on the steps with Monique sitting between my legs.

When two dudes got out and headed up toward us, I looked down at Monique with a smirk on my face, and asked her, "Is this your man and his partner? They look upset." Instead of answering, she gave me a light elbow to my leg.

"Nique, anymore ribs in the house?" The driver asked as they approached.

"Yup."

"Good. I'm hungry as a hostage. What's up dog?" He said, looking at me, "I'm Brian, and this is my partna', Lace," he said, as we shook hands, and I acknowledged his mans with a slight nod.

"Tay. And that's my man Sig."

"Shid, I was startin' to think that Nique be lyin' when she'd be gon' on her little trips. I guess you like to keep a low profile."

"You know how shit be. Keeping the finances intact is time consuming. I been wanting to get down here, to not only see my baby," I said, kissing her on the forehead, "but to holla at choo. She told me you be doing what choo do."

"I be doing a lil sumin'."

Nodding my head, I told him, "Aiight, tomorrow we'll hook up and kick it."

"That'll work."

*****

Sig and Karmel were following me and Mo as we left from having breakfast at a black owned family restaurant.

"Baby, once we talk to the people about these buildings, we goin' down to Atlanta for the weekend, do a little shoppin', a lot a fucking and parlay."

"That sounds good," Mo said, rubbing the back of my head. Then she asked me, "Baby, what if we can't get both spots?"

"What choo most interested in?"

"I really want the shop, but the beauty supply store will profit faster, 'cause I don't have a large clientele."

"Profits aren't as important as being happy and enjoying what choo do. I know you will eventually get it pumping and you ain't gon' be wantin' fa shit. So, put your energy into building what choo want. These type…"

Pointing straight ahead, Mo told me, "make a left at that light and it's the pet store on the left hand side."

The store was owned by an old white lady who was ready to close it down. She said she'd only kept it open because her husband had started the business, but since he'd passed away, she wasn't interested in keeping it going. A more than generous offer was going to get us that spot. I decided to let Mo deal with the shop first and see how that goes. The property on the out skirts of town was an old tire factory, so it was spacious enough for the slaughterhouse. I decided that I'd talk to an attorney, and let him, or her, negotiate the deal. Now, all that was left, before we could leave for Atlanta, was for me to holla at dude.

"Baby, call Brian and tell 'im to meet us at the house. I figure that I can kick it wit' him then we can leave tomorrow."

"Okay."

By the time we got back to Mo's spot, he was already there sitting in the car smoking a blunt. He got out when we pulled up, and we all went in the house. I led Mo into the bedroom, gave her $3,500.00 and told her, "Go see what's Victoria's newest secret. And while you're out, get me some blunts."

"Alright. How much time you need?"

"By the time you finish doing that, we'll be through talking."

"Okay, I'll be back in a few." She said, leaving the bedroom, and heading for the door, said, "K, lets roll out."

I went into the living room. "So, Bee, how shit be goin' 'round here?" I asked as soon as the ladies were gone.

"It's some money down here. The police don't really phuck wit' choo unless shit is wild and loud. The hoods that I mainly be in is straight, 'cause the neighbors mind their business and the blue unies don't be deep."

"What slabs go for down here?" Sig asked.

"If you know the right people, you can get 'em fa 22-5." Sig didn't smile outright, but I saw the skin on his forehead raise, and I knew he was as elated as I was.

After I glanced at him, I asked Brian, "Is there a lot of cats that's getting' 'em to the point where they're the only ones who can sho' love wit' da yay?"

"My man I be phuckin' wit' be on more than anybody else I done phucked wit', and his prices don't be high, but they ain't low either. Anybody who selling birds, prices be 'bout da same. So, to answer yo question, I'd have to say, naw, not no one person."

"If you get 'bout five, they still 22, 22-5?" Sig asked.

"I don't know. I only be gettin' one or one and a half at the most."

Trying to see where his head was at, I asked him, "If you got 20 or 25 of 'em, on a regular, what would you push 'em fa?"

His eyes widened, and the part of his smile that couldn't be hidden broke through and was visible. He looked at us, and asked, "What I'd be gettin' 'em fa?"

"15-5," I answered.

"I'd push 'em fa 18-5. Long as I'm always on, they can get 'em fa da low-low."

His last sentence said a lot about his hustling mentality, and I was ready to see what he could do.

"Well, dig, I'll get choo 25 down here when I get back from Atlanta. As long as you ain't bullshitin', it won't stop. It'll only get better."

Monique and Karmel got back about an hour and a half after we finished talking, and Brian had gone.

"Wake up sleepy." I heard Monique say, right before she gave me a light kiss on the lips. I rose up and looked over at Sig. He had fallen asleep on the couch.

"Dem damn trees knocked me da phuck out."

"You ain't bullshitin'," he said, laying back with his arm rested over his eyes. Karmel lifted his head, sat down, and nestled it in her lap.

"Yall hittin' the A-T-L wit' us?" Mo asked, looking toward the couch.

Sig wasn't big on that couples shit. Had it been two women we had both just met, and we're just going out of town to hang out, I would have expected him to say, "yeah." But knowing that Mo was more than a fuck thang for me, I figured he wasn't trying to get caught up in no intimate couple rendezvous.

Karmel was looking down at him when he said, "I want to, bad as hell. But, I gotta get back home." He raised up and looked at me, then continued, "You already done had me put shit on hold 'cause you didn't wanna ride down her by yourself. I can't prolong it no longer, regardless of how much I want too."

"I forgot all about that," I said. "Well, let me brush my grill and then we can get up outta this house."

While I was brushing my teeth, I was standing in front of the toilet about to piss when Mo came in. She reached around me and grabbed my tool and said, "Let me hold this for you."

"Thank you," I said, and kept brushing my teeth.

"I got a nice spot we gon' hit"

"What's the dress code?"

"Dress to sweat," she said, shaking my man and putting him back in my pants.

*****

We went to a club called Luxuries. It must have been one of Dayton's elite clubs, 'cause all the people were flashing.

In a pair of Sean John blue jean shorts with a white Sean John tee shirt and some white Rockports, my attire was simple. But the platinum Cartier watch with the frozen face, the platinum 26 inch Cartier link with the iced out Old English D, that I always wear when I'm outta town, and the three carat solitaire Cartier platinum ring on my left pinkie was talking loud. Not to mention the 5'5" chocolate bombshell on my arm.

Mo was looking luscious! Her long black hair was lying flat on her head and falling on her shoulders like strips of silk. She had a two carat pink diamond on her ring finger that matched the 5 carat pink diamond necklace and 2.5 carat ankle bracelet that I had bought her for Sweetest Day. I couldn't be mad at all the eyes that were glued to her big ole' ass. It was banging in them denim Baby Phat shorts, and the cleavage from those C cup melons were eye catching in the white

Baby Phat tank top. All that was supported by a pair of slightly bow legs and beautifully pedicured feet that rested in a pair of two tone Ostrich slide ins.

Ashanti's *Baby* was filling the club when we walked in. A benji got us a table in the V.I.P section. Sig ordered two fifths of Courvoisier and two fifths of HPNOTIQ as soon as we sat down. When the waitress brought the bottles, she poured me and Sig yak and the ladies glasses of Hypno. Sig raised his glass and we all followed suit. "To a night wit' beautiful women and a night wit' my best boy."

"My man," I said, and tossed back my first shot.

After about four more shots and the sound of Jay-Z's *Dirt Off Ya Shoulder*, I grabbed Mo's hand and led her to the dance floor. She started off dancing like we had just met.

"Back that shit up, girl!"

"Oh, you want a bitch to get nasty," she said, moving to the beat. I just nodded my head with a devilish grin on my face. "I didn't wanna embarrass you, 'cause I can shake this muthaphucka," she said, as she slapped her ass.

"Well shake it then! Gangstas don't get embarrassed on the flo'. They profile on the flo like this," I threw my hands in the air and started rocking to the beat, "and let their dame shake that money maker."

Sig and Karmel were next to us, and apparently she knew what she was supposed to be doing. She was bent over shaking it up and Sig was slapping that ass to the beat. Mo was really doing her thang too. And it got even better when *Welcome to Atlanta* came on. She dropped down and came up slow, like she was sizing me up. Then she reached back and put her arms around my neck and started rolling her hips and sliding up and down. By the time I pulled her close to me, so we could slow dance, when Jagged Edge' *I Promise* came on. We were both sweatin', and I was hard as a rock.

Looking down into her eyes, I told her, "You know you got it coming tonight, don't choo."

"You promise?"

"I promise," I said, and leaned down to kiss her.

Chapter Twenty

"Baby, I'm hungry."

"And what's new? You hungry all day, every day," Rome said. "What choo want?"

I got a taste for a corned beef sandwich on a onion roll, with coleslaw, American and Swiss cheese on it. Then let's go for a walk. The doctor said if I exercise while I'm pregnant, it'll be easier for me to regain my shape."

Rome looked at her and said, "Well, we'll go eat at Lou's Deli, then go downtown and do some walking on Belle Isle. And, hopefully you won't be too tired to hangout wit' me tonight."

*****

They were riding down Six Mile when Rome received a disturbing call. Landa looked over at him when she heard him say, "How long he been in jail?" After a slight pause, he said, "What's his bond? Why ain't nobody go get 'im? Phuck, what it cost? And give 'im his usual so he can do him."

Rome flipped his phone shut and tossed it in Landa's lap. Then he started rubbing her stomach and talking, "Remember to always use common sense. If you don't have common sense, then no other sense matters."

Landa put her hand over his, looked at him and said, "This is our baby, not one of those knuckle heads that work for you. Our baby is going to have damn good sense."

"You're right," he said, as they pulled into the parking lot at Lou's.

Once they left the deli, instead of going downtown, they went to Mumford High School to walked.

"I remember being in this blue muthaphucka as a freshman," Rome said, as they made their third lap around the track. "You, Tasha, Trina and the rest of your girls were the fly girls." He continued, "and I always thought you looked the best. And you knew I had a crush on you too."

"Yeah, I knew. You was a mannish lil boy too. You were cute, but just cute, 'cause you were too young. We wanted older boys that were out of school. You see, Tay had Tasha gon'."

"Damn, they have been together forever. It's damn near the end of 2003. They started phuckin' 'round in '92. Like EnVogue said, Tay held on to his love." He grabbed her hand, looked at her and said, "And I'm a follow his lead."

"You better."

By the time they finished walking and talking Landa was exhausted. When they got home, Rome told her to lay down and take a nap.

"I'll call and wake you up, so you can start getting dressed, on my way back home."

"Where you going?

I gotta run a few errands, but it won't take long, so you better go 'head and lay down."

"Okay. Be careful," she said, and kissed him.

Rome called a cat that he does business with as soon as he pulled out of the driveway. "I'm on my way. I should be there in about 15 minutes," he said, and hung up.

On the way to his final destination, he stopped at Junior's after hour spot. When he pulled up at the back door, he called and hollered at Junior for a minute. About two minutes later, the door opened and a young dude, about 22 stepped out with a .40 cal in his hand and looked around. He turned around and waved to *come on* to somebody in the club. A second later, another young cat came out carrying two green duffle bags. Without a word, he opened the back door of Landa's BMW X5, and put them in, and Rome pulled off.

He made another stop at a house about four streets over from the after hour spot. He grabbed the two bags and as soon as he unlocked the armored gate and the door, he was met by two brown pit bulls. They were jumping all over him. When he turned off the alarm, he closed the door and carried the duffle bags to the back room, where there were already brown paper bags on the floor. He let the dogs out in the backyard while he cleaned up their shit, mopped the basement floor and put out some food and fresh water. Once he finished with his menial tasks, he let the dogs back into the house, locked up and headed to his final stop.

It took Rome about 15 minutes to reach his destination. He pulled into the driveway of a house on Appoline off Six Mile, and hit his horn. Out of the house came a light skinned, short cat about Rome's age. He got in the truck and gave Rome a play.

"Good looking out Rome," he said. "I needed to get on bad."

Rome reached in the back seat and retrieved the grocery store bag and handed it to him. "E, that's two right here. I'm givin' 'em to you 'cause you have looked out for me in the past. But, I'm a be truthful wit' choo, dog, I had my reservations 'bout this 'cause niggas told me you was workin' wit' those people.

E started shaking his head and told Rome, "Muthaphuckas said that shit 'cause the hook hit my crib and found half a slab, but I beat that shit. And the reason I beat it is 'cause their warrant was for boy and not cane. Plus, it was the state, not the Feds."

Rome just nodded his head and said, "Aiight. Well, get at me when you finish."

"Bet," he said, and got out the truck.

Rome called Landa as he was pulling out of the driveway and headed home.

As soon as he got home, he jumped in the shower. When he got out, Landa was already dressed. He looked at her and gave a love whistle. Clad in a crème Gucci dress and a pair of peanut butter Iguana skin shoes, she was simply beautiful.

Once dressed, decked out in a black Oxford suit, white Oxford shirt, and a pair of black cleverly Norwegian lace-ups, Rome looked the part of a King ready to accompany his Queen out for a night on the town.

Rome decided to dine at Coco's Comedy Kitchen. The food was good and the entertainment was off the hook. Walking in, Landa saw Tone and Trina, and made her way toward them. Accustomed to getting what he wants, Rome dropped a couple of C-notes on one of the waitresses and the four of them were led to a front table by the stage. Once seated, Rome looked around to check out his surroundings. He noted that Tommy Hearns was in the house, as well as NBA Finals MVP, Chauncey Billups, and a few other Detroit big shots.

"If yall will excuse me, I have to use the restroom," he said. Tone gave him an inquiring look, but with a light shake of the head, Rome let him know that everything was all right.

Landa looked at Trina and asked her, "Have you talked to Tasha today?'

"Yeah, I talked to her earlier. Since Tay is outta town, I called 'er before I got dressed to see if she wanted to come wit' me and Tone. But she said that she was going to take Lil Tay to see 'Nemo'."

Right before she got ready to ask another question, she saw Rome talking to some man, and it looked like he passed him some money also.

They all sat there eating, drinking red wine, and listening to the comics. A new comic came on stage and everybody thought he was hilarious. Landa noticed that he was the man she'd seen Rome talking to. The man at the table next to them was the butt of his last few jokes. Then, before she knew it, he was staring at their table. "Dig this here, Brother, why you looking at me like that?" Now it seemed like every eye in the club on was on them. "What? You think you can be more entertaining than me?"

Landa turned and looked at Rome as he said, "To some."

"Well come on up here wit' cha bad ass. Fly Guy. Everybody give Ron O'Neal a round of applause."

The crowd started clapping as Rome made his way to the stage and got the microphone.

"First of all," he said, standing on stage, "I realize that it takes a lot of heart to do this. But, it's what has my heart," he continued, as he walked toward his table, "that's given me the courage to do this. Yolanda Madison," he said, as the spotlight shun on their table. "I love you so much that I want to spend the rest of my life wit' choo," he said, as he reached into his inside pocket and retrieved the black velvet ring box and proceeded to kneel on one knee.

Trina's hands covered her mouth as she leaned her head on Tone. He hugged her and they sat there smiling.

When Rome flipped open the box, the comedian that gave him the mic yelled out, "Bling Muthaphuckin' Bling!

With her hands still covering her mouth, Trina kinda fell back like she'd been looking at a horror movie at the sight of the 5 carat platinum emerald-cut engagement ring.

"Will you marry me?" Rome asked, staring up into the teary eyes of Landa.

She was speechless. Frantically nodding her head up and down, she managed to say, "Yes," as her and Rome stood to embrace.

He gave her a light kiss on the lips, then mouthed, "I love you," as he wiped the tears that were streaming down her face.

Chapter Twenty-One

"Thanks for coming on such short notice."

"RaTasha, you know I'd stop the world from spinning if it'll get us in the same place at the same time," Alex said, as he sat down at the bar. Tasha had called Alex early in the day and arranged to meet him at 7:00 p.m. at Carlo's Lounge.

"You look beautiful, as usual," he continued. "I was beginning to think that you weren't going to call me."

"Alex, this is not a social visit in the sense that you think. I needed to talk to you about that stunt you pulled last week at the club. That was very disrespectful."

"To you?"

" To my man," she said, voice full of attitude.

"Phuck your man! Who is that nigga that I gotta respect him. Look, I don't wanna get choo in trouble, but I don't like the way things ended between us. And if I didn't believe that you cared about me, I wouldn't have went through such lengths to get in touch wit' choo."

"Alex, you know I cared about you. But I needed to make a clean break. I apologize for not being up front and honest with you. Tay is home, I love my man and that's who I'm a be wit'."

He reached across the table and put his hand over hers, and in a low voice he said, "Mini me." She looked at him. "Who are you trying to convince? I know I'm the man who makes you smile and makes your toes curl. I also remember me being the man that you trusted enough to let your son hang out wit', at my nephew's birthday party, while you studied for exams. Don't throw that away 'cause dude is home and can buy you a nice watch. Cats like that might do all right for a minute, but they fall. Men like me are untouchable, and built to last. And you epitomize everything that I desire and deserve in a woman."

Tasha pulled her hand away, reached for her purse and stood up. "I'm not going to leave him," she said, and walked out.

Being in the car, riding by herself was therapeutic her. She began to think about how wonderful life was now that Tay was home. And in retrospect, she knew that she came close to throwing it all away. Had she accepted Alex's marriage proposal, she would have regretted it. Or would she? She thought to herself. "Shake these thoughts girl. Alex is a thing of the past," she said aloud, as she pulled her phone out of her purse to call Landa, and tell her she was on her way by.

As soon as she flipped the phone closed, it rang. "My Love, I miss you," Tay said, as soon as she answered.

"I miss you too, Baby. When you coming home? I'm sick of sleeping alone."

"I'll be home in a couple of days. What choo into?"

"Me and mama went to dinner, an' I just dropped her off. Now, I'm on my way over to Landa's for a minute. Tay wanted to stay wit' his Papa."

"Well you be careful. You know I don't like you to be out late."

"I know. And I'm going straight home when I leave there."

"Aiight. I just called to check-in, and let choo know that you can be expecting me in the next day or two."

"Okay. I love you, and you be careful too."

"Always, and I love you too."

Chapter Twenty-Two

"Tash, lets hit Floods tonight."

"Boo, I don't really wanna hangout tonight. How 'bout I cook us a nice dinner and we stay home."

"Whateva; you want. You're the boss."

I looked at her as she left outta the room and could sense that something was wrong. I kinda figured that she was upset that I stayed gone longer than I said I would. But then again, she knows that there's no telling what I might have to do. Since the food wasn't going to be ready for an hour or so, I decided to go holla at my lil brother. I called Rome and told him that I was on my way over.

Tash was at the island in the kitchen beating the steaks when I walked in. I walked up behind her, wrapped my arms around her and kissed her on the back of the neck.

"I like when you do that," she said.

"I know what choo like. I been knowing what choo like since you were 17."

After I grabbed me a corona out of the fridge, I told her, "I'll be right back. I gotta shoot up to Dibo's for a minute."

"Don't be gone long."

"I won't," I said, and gave her a light kiss on the forehead.

*****

Landa answered the door when I arrived at their house. "What's up stranger? When you get back?" She asked me, as I walked in.

"The other day. What's up wit' choo?"

"Just living and getting bigger."

"You silly. Where's my man at?"

"Jerome is not my man." The smile left my face and was replaced with a look of confusion. "He's my fiancé'," she told me, flashing her ring.

"Damn! Congratulations. I'm happy for yall."

"Thank you. He's downstairs in the basement."

The sounds of Jaheim were blaring as I walked down the steps. Rome was shooting pool when I said, "Bet fifty push-ups you miss that duck."

He looked up. "My man, what' up? When you get back?"

"The other day," I answered, giving him a play and a hug. "But what's up wit' choo, mister engaged. Congratulations."

With a big stupid grin on his face, he said, "Thanks. It was time. I'm hooked and don't want nobody but her."

"I feel you. Wish my number one relationship was on point like that."

He gave me a quizzical look and said, "Hold on, I'll be back." He went in the back room and came back carrying two Coronas. He handed me one and sat on the couch opposite me. "Now, what's up wit' choo and Tasha?"

"I've been having a gut feeling that something is up, and the feeling isn't good. She seems so distant. And it just started 'bout a month or so ago."

"You think she knows about Monique?

"I doubt it. I was thinking that maybe I've been slacking. But when I got here it became apparent that it ain't me."

"Why you say that?"

"Dog, I done been home two days and she ain't tell me that you and Landa was engaged. And I know she know."

"Yeah, she know," Rome said, nodding his head nonchalantly.

"Okay then. That means that something has her distracted. And I bet I'm a press the shit outta her when I get home. Something is up. She ain't wanna go out tonight. Her moods been different. Even Tay noticed it.

"The other day when I got home, I was wrestling wit' him. Usually they'll jump on me, yunno." Rome nodded his head. "But she just sat on the porch wit' a bullshitin' smile on her face. So Tay run over to her, grab her hand and try to pull 'er up, but she shakes her head no. He like, 'what's wrong mama?' She don't say nothing, and give 'im a kiss. At that point, I'm just figuring that she mad 'cause I had been gone so long."

"You was gone a while! Did you have fun?"

"Always, when I'm wit' that girl. Mo be making it hard for me to leave. I don't never say it, but I love the shit outta her. And, I'll tell you sumin' else, let me find out Tash done phucked up, and Mo will get a gift fa her left ring finger."

"Dog, I can't see Tasha doing nothing that'll jeopardize yalls relationship. But one things fa sho', you and Tay ain't both wrong in yalls assessment of yalls girl."

"Naw, we ain't," I said, shaking my head and standing up so I could leave. "I gotta stop at Dibo's and take a quick inventory of the liquor. To be a club owner, I don't know what be going on up there. I just check the books and make sure the deposits be made."

"Hey, that's the important shit. If it's turning a profit, it's straight. And it ain't losing money, so Marcel must be a helluva manager."

"Well. Let me get outta here. I gotta go interrogate this bitch. I hope I don't have to kill 'er."

Rome busted out laughing. "Please don't do that!"

I started laughing myself. "I ain't, dog. I'm straight."

"Aiight. Love ya, dog."

"Love you too."

On my way home, I stopped at my club. It was only about 7:00 p.m., and it didn't open til nine. That gave me enough time to go in and take inventory of all the supplies that I needed. Me and Marcel went over the books, kicked some ideas around, placed a few orders, then I left.

On the ride home, I started wondering if I'd been so engrossed in my business that I missed the signs of her unhappiness. And that led to her doing something that'll tear us apart. When I walked in the house, I called out to Tash.

"I'm in here." I heard her voice answer as she was coming from the study. "Your plate is in the microwave. It should still be warm. I just put it in there."

"Aiight," I said, heading toward the kitchen.

I got my plate and went in the study to join Tash. She was curled up on the butter soft leather couch reading the *The Hustlers Wife*, by Nikki Turner.

"Well this is somethin' I've never seen in all the years we've been together," I said, as I sat down at the desk. Shooing Tara away, I yelled, "Go sit down," then I looked at Tash and asked her, "Why you ain't tell me Rome and Landa were engaged?"

She looked up from the book and shrugged her shoulder's. "Shit, I just forgot."

"What's weighing so heavily on your mind that your moods have changed? And don't tell me nothing. Somethin' is up and I'd like to know what it is."

I put my fork down and went and sat on the couch with her. Placing her feet in my lap I said, "Boo you haven't been yourself. What's up?"

Tash laid the book in her lap and looked up at me. Her look was that of a child who was doing something to please their parents, and it gave me an uneasy feeling. I began to nervously wonder if she had done something and the guilt was starting to get to her, or if Monique had called like she so often threatened.

"What's up Baby? What's on your mind?" I asked.

"Nuttin'. I've just missed you. Earlier I was looking at all these books that you have, and love reading, so I figured I'd start reading too. And what better one to start with then this one," she said, as she held the book up so that I could see the cover.

"That book was good as hell! But dude was a little too forgiving for me."

Tash dropped her head and looked at the book for a minute then looked back up at me and said, "Well I don't know what she did, yet, but I know that I'd forgive you for any mistakes that you might make. And I hope that you'd do the same for me."

Something in the way she said that let me know that she wasn't hypothetically speaking, and I wanted to know what she was talking about.

"Aiight Tash lets cut thru the bullshit! What have you done? I know I've been gone a lot, and we haven't been spending much time together lately. And I say that to say that I can accept my part in whateva has happened. But whateva it is you must tell me now, so that we can start puttin' this behind us." As I kept talking, tears began to roll down her face. The fact her conscience was eating at her like that actually scared me. "We've been together too long," I continued, "to let one mistake ruin us."

"Tay I swear it only happened once," she said, clutchin the pillow to her chest.

"Tash tell me you haven't been creeping when I'm out of town. And please tell me you haven't fucked one of my friends!"

She sat there clutching the pillow and shaking her head from side to side before she looked at me and said, "No, no. I would never betray you like that."

The words 'like that' instantly upset me. "But you are admitting to betraying me in some way?" I asked, my voice dripping with resentment.

"Its not like you…"

"Cut the bullshit!" I yelled. "The game is over. What da phuck have you done!"

Tash looked up at me and bit down on her lower lip. I stared at her with a mixture of hurt and hate in my eyes, knowing that I was about to hear what every in love man dreads. We stared at each other until she finally began to speak.

"While you were locked up I met this guy, who I rejected at first. But he kept pursuing me and I was lonely as hell, and baby I fell weak to his advances. I'm sorry!" I stood up and started pacing. "I'm even sorrier that I didn't tell you who it is."

At the completion of her last sentence I stopped pacing, looked at her and asked, "What choo mean is?"

Sitting up on the couch, staring straight ahead with her hands in her lap she said, "The guy's name is Alex."

"Wait a minute. Who the phuck is Alex? Are you still phuckin' wit 'im? And that's why you're acting all distant all of a sudden."

Crying uncontrollably she shook her head no. "Well why you telling me this niggas' name, like I know 'im?" I asked, standing in front of her.

She looked up at me and said, "Cause he's the one that sent the drinks when we were at the club that night."

"Bitch! You done lost your mind! You done allowed this nigga to make me look like a damn fool!" I yelled, and slapped her with as much might as I could muster.

Tash fell back and shrieked, "What was I supposed to do!"

"You was 'spose to tell me to send that shit back and tell me what was up," I yelled. "Yeah, I'd a been pissed, but you don't let nobody make a fool of me. Unless you ain't... Neva mind. Phuck it! And phuck you," I said, leaving the room. Without looking back I grabbed my keys off the hall hook and left.

****

"Would you bring me anotha double of Courvoisier?" I asked the waitress, when she came to collect the other shot glasses from my table.

When I left the house I jumped in my truck and started riding. I ended up downtown and was hungry, since I didn't finish eating at home. So I hit Chocolate City, and ordered me a steak. Tash had called me at least a dozen times, that's why when my phone rang I almost ignored it. But I looked at the caller I.D. and saw Rome's number.

"I'm aiight." I said when answered.

"Where you at?"

"At Chocolate City. I don't know for how long doe. My eye has just been caught by a bad muthaphucka."

"Man I'm on my way down there."

"Aiight."

When I flipped my phone closed the mocha stallion that I'd made eye contact with was strolling toward my table. She was every bit of 6'0" tall with cornrolls going to the back. Her titties weren't real big, but the ass that she was toting rivaled the girl in the Outkast video. As she approached I stood and pulled a chair out for her.

She looked at me with beautiful jade green eyes, and said, "Thank you."

My first thoughts were that she was wearing contacts. But the thought evaporated at the sound of her Jamaican accent.

"What choo drinking?" I asked.

"Unfortunately me not stay for drinks. Me and my friends enjoy the steaks here and were finishing up when I saw you on the phone. So, I waited until you got off so me could meet choo."

"Well I'm flattered I must say. I'm Tay. What's yo name?"

"Shanice," she said, and proceeded to write numbers on a napkin. Handing it to me she continued, "and these are my contact numbers. Feel free to use them anytime." She stood to leave. "My friends are in the car waiting, but I'll be expecting your call."

Standing as well, I asked, "How 'bout I call you later on tonight?"

With a thousand watt smile on her face she said, "Anytime."

I winked at her, and said, "Gotcha gorgeous."

I watched her strut out the door and smiled at the explicit thoughts that crossed my mind. Rome arrived about 15 minutes later. He sat down and ordered a shot of Quevo.

"Tasha came over to the house crying an shit. When I seen 'er all distraught I knew something was wrong. That's when I called you. What happened?"

I filled him in on the events that took place. How I was able to extract the info from her. How I lost my temper and slapped her for the first time.

"Dog, we been together for over eleven years. This is the first time I ever got so mad that I put my hands on 'er, but I don't feel bad."

"You shouldn't. I mean... She phucked around while you were gone...shit happens. But to allow you to be played like that was foul. What choo gon' do?"

"Stay da phuck away from her for a while. I'll probably go down to Mo's and delve around in their market. Get the slaughterhouse up and running, and put shit down."

The waitress came by and Rome told her to bring him a fifth of Quevo. The joint was starting to liven up and more girls were making themselves seen. After a few shots of Quevo and seeing all of that ass shaking, my spirits were up, and I was in party mode. Balling up twenty-dollar bills throwing them at the girls on stage. Getting lap dances. Before long we had five or six females at our table dancing with us and each other. I got up to go to the bathroom. On my way back I saw some niggas at our table. One of the dudes and Rome appeared to be having some words. I immediately made my way over there.

"What's the problem dog?" I asked Rome, but stared at dude.

"It looks like the HATERS came out tonight," Rome answered.

"Haters! Yall ain't the only niggas getting money. My whole team getting paid. PHUCK MCN!"

With that statement I blinked out. No more words were spoken. I socked the dude right in the face, and we proceeded to tear the club up. Security started grabbing and macing cats. In the midst of the commotion I looked to see if I could see Rome, then everything went black.

I awoke at Harper Grace Hospital with a headache, and a light being shined into my eyes. "Well, Mr. Manning, you have a mild concussion to go with the stitches."

"Stitches?" I asked.

The doctor nodded his head and said, "Yup. You had a nasty gash on the corner of your right eye brow that required eight stitches. It'll leave a little scar, but you won't be disfigured. You may have a headache for a few days. Get some aspirin and you'll be fine." I nodded my head okay. "Any questions?"

"Naw. I'm just ready to go home and get some rest."

"Well young man make sure you do get some rest, and you're all set."

In the waiting room waiting when I walked out was Rome and Sig. Rome's clothes were torn and his lip was swollen, but he didn't look like he had gotten the shortest end of the stick in the club brawl. I assured them that I'd feel better once we finished them off.

"After the chaos died down them niggas were still there. Rome called me while he was driving you to the spital. I had a crew from Southwest go see what was up. You know hoes will give you the low down just to be gossiping, and for a few dollars they'll give up everything else they know."

"So what were they able to find out?"

"The one that cracked choo wit' the bottle was still there wit' one of his mans. Of course Tico and 'nem got them niggas trunk bound and too 'em to the house on Vernon. I figured you'd wanna handle dude personally."

I started shaking my head and told Sig, "Its not personal. They'll be used as examples. But I do wanna know what crew their wit', and start wiping 'nem out. These niggas' 'bout ta learn that MCN runs this muthaphuckin' City! We giving these bitch ass niggas off water prices and they gon' start showin' respect, or pass form."

We followed Rome to his house. He parked his car in the driveway and got in the car with me and Sig. "Lil Tee came up to the spital. I gave 'im your keys so he could go pick up your ride. He gon' park it in your driveway and put the keys in the mailbox," he told me as we headed to Southwest Detroit.

Once we got to the Southwest house the two cats were eager to tell us they were down with the Township Crew. I guess they thought that would scare us and we'd let them go. WRONG! I ordered for them to be tortured until locations of other crew members houses, safe houses and any other information was given. After the information was received they were to be brutally murdered and left in Clark Park on Clark and Vernon.

Chapter Twenty-Three

"Baby you watching the news? These niggas' out here losing they minds," Landa said, walking into the den.

"What they doin'?"

"They just found two men dead, with brooms broke off in their rectums in an alley on the Eastside. We might need to move down south or something. There's been a lot of killing in the last month. Whole families have been murdered. Kids and everythang."

Rome pulled her down into his lap and told her, "Baby, you know we have these killing sprees every year. Don't worry. It'll stop. But I don't want choo in the streets at night. And when you go somewhere let me know."

The doorbell rang and Landa gave Rome a light kiss on the lips. "Okay." She said, as she stood up. "Its probably for you. I'm going upstairs to take a shower. If you can get rid of whoever it is at the door, you should come join me."

"I just might do that," he said, and gave her a smack on the ass as he went to answer the door.

When Rome looked thru the peephole and saw Tay and Sig his antenna went up. The looks on their faces told him that this was not a social visit. "What up doe," he said when he opened the door.

They both gave him a play and a brotherly embrace as they stepped in the house, but remained silent.

He looked at Sig and asked, "What's up?"

"C'mon," he said, as he followed Tay into the den.

Rome closed the door behind them and said, "Now what's up? Yall walk in here all quiet and shit. What's da deal?"

Tay and Sig looked at each other. Sig dropped his head. Tay turned his focus to Rome and said, "They killed Lil Tee last night. Him and Rob was at Club Network. When they left some niggas' gunned 'em down at they ride. Rob took shots, but he strait."

With a look of anger Rome asked, "How he live and Tee died?"

"We just left Receiving Hospital. Aside from checking on him I knew you'd wanna know what happened. He said they was approaching Tee's ride when he heard gun shots. He said he kinda ducked and when he looked 'round he seen two cats walking toward them bussing. He said when he saw Tee sprawled on the hood he tried to get 'im, but he got hit and went down. He said he guess they thought they was both done, cause the shooting stopped. And when he got up and walked to the front of the car, Tee was laid out wit' two holes in his face."

"Where he get shot at?" Rome asked.

"In his chest, and in his shoulder."

Rome sat down and laid his head back staring at the ceiling. Sig looked at Tay and asked him, "What other info did you get? You said you'd tell me when we hook up."

"Oh yeah! I figured that dem niggas' were a part of somethin' bigger to had been able to survive the onslaught we put down after that shit jumped off. I was right. They plugged in wit' Grease, Bo, and them dudes off the Eastside. It's quite a few of 'em in Highland Park too. They call themselves G.N.'s, a.k.a. Grimey Niggas."

"Damn," Sig said, "I thought me and Bo was aiight."

"Yall was until we fell out wit' his peoples. If you fallout wit' a muthaphucka I'm aiight wit' my attitude is gon' be phuck that nigga," Tay said.

"Yeah, you right. I'm feeling that," Sig responded, nodding his head.

Rome became excited. "Phuck them niggas! It's time to go all out," he yelled, standing up.

Tay held his hands up to calm him down. "Look Rome," he began "you're speaking out of anger right now, which is understandable. But to react out of anger would be foolish. An angry man can't think, and a man that can't think won't be worth the dirt that he's buried up under. I'm in the process of acquiring some important info. Once I find out everythang we need to know I'll fill yall in, and we gon' end this shit. Until then, lay low and be extra careful when you do business."

Tay and Sig left, and Rome sat in the den thinking about Lil Tee. Tee had been like his little brother every since he first met him. Rome could still hear the voice of the kid who walked up to him over Nikki's house and said, "I wanna get paid, and I'm down fa whateva."

Lil Tee was 12 when Rome was fucking his cousin Nikki. At the time Rome was 16, and getting work from Tay to keep money in his pocket. But Tee used to be with him all the time. Then by the time Tay started giving Rome some weight to play with, Tee was 14 and got his first sack. He had always been loyal to Rome and very trustworthy. The thought of Tee saying, "Kid or senior citizen O.G., no witness is going to do you in," brought tears to Rome's eyes.

He had his face in his hands silently weeping when Landa walked into the room. "What's wrong baby?" She asked, standing in front of him and rubbing the back of his head.

He looked up at her and told her, "Lil Tee got killed last night."

Knowing how close they were, she just cradled his head into her stomach, and said, "It'll be alright."

****

Dibo's was full of MCN affiliates two days after Lil Tee's funeral. Most of the discussions were about how deep the police had been in the neighborhoods.

"This beef is phuckin' shit up!" Junior was telling Rome as they sat in Tay's office talking. "My Eastside spots have been doing what they do, but shits been hot on this side of town. Them dudes gotta go."

"I don't know what's been on my brothers mind. He's being too patient. They done knocked off a few of our mans, and we get theirs when we catch 'em slipping. What kinda shit is that?"

"What Sig saying?" Junior asked.

"That same bullshit my brotha be talking. Just chill and be patient, it'll be over in a minute."

"Well, we'll be patient then. This is family, and dude ain't gonna make no decisions that'll hurt us. You know that." Rome nodded his head in agreement. "The joint teaches you the benefits of being patient.

"You can fallout wit' a dude in the mess hall and react and end up wit' an inciting a riot ticket, fighting or an assault ticket and sit in the hole for a minute. Or you could be in the same situation and lay back and put a play together. The result being, the adversary gets handled and you don't have any problems from him or the institution."

"Well I'll learn patience thru yall. Phuck going to da joint."

They sat back kicking it and smoking a blunt. When the door opened, Rome was not only surprised at who entered, but he was not ready for the litany of questions he knew she was about to ask.

"Where's he at Rome?"

"Tasha I ain't seen 'im or talked to 'im since the other day at the funeral."

"I'm a start clearing these cats out so we can leave when you finish," Junior said, as he left out.

"Rome its been over three weeks, and I haven't heard from him. Is he coming back home? He won't return my calls. When he drops Tay off, he just pulls off as soon as the front door opens."

"Tasha I don't know what he's planning to do. I know he's phucked up 'bout what happened, but he doesn't talk 'bout it. I pick up Tay when he asks me too, and that's it."

"Where's he staying at?"

"You know I can't tell you that."

"Well when you see him, please tell him that I love him, and I need to talk to him."

"I will. And Tasha, be careful. Shit is thick now."

"I figured that. He got some muthaphucka that's been following me." Rome just smiled. Even though Tay was pissed at her, his brother always covered all bases.

Chapter Twenty-Four

The last few weeks couldn't have been any better for me. I was able to attain all the information I needed to handle the beef we were in. Rome thought I was going soft, but after I finish laying my plan out to him and Sig he'll realize that I'm only getting wiser.

When I pulled into the parking lot at Dibo's there were only two cars in it. Rome's white 600 SL and Sig's black Impala SS. We went in and sat at the bar. I got right down to business.

"Sig, you know I be hollering at Ito."

"Strait up! What's that fool into?"

"Same ole shit. He's over there on the East Coast handling some thangs. That boy is paying his luxury tax, and we gon' hook up wit' 'im on that tip. But right now he's gon' assist us in this beef."

"Who is Ito?" Rome asked.

"One of our mans from the joint."

"How is he going to assist us?" Sig asked.

"I've found out the whereabouts of the GN workers, who pluggin' 'im, and the locations of where the head men lay their heads, wit' their families. Ito is sending a crew this way that we'll hook up wit' some of our people. By us having been so patient they probably figure that we're hoes, and don't want it wit' them. They've become laxed, and that's why they won't survive this attack."

Sig took a swig of his beer and looked at me smiling. "I like that," he said. "This way they can knock these dudes off and head East."

"That's right," I said. "And now is not the time to have a conscience, cause when we hit they houses, everybody goes." Nodding my head I continued, "That's the way its goin' down."

****

A couple of weeks before Thanksgiving Yahmo called and asked me to meet him in **Sin City**. I hadn't been to Vegas in a while, so a trip to the desert didn't seem bad at all. We had all but stuck a fork in the war with the GN cats. Actually the war was lopsided. Our losses were minimal and we got our point across to all who looked on, and might've had thoughts of trying to be our equals. The streets of Detroit understood that you either rolled with MCN, or shared in the fate of our enemies.

My flight gave me a chance to think about the success of my organization. We had our hand in everything in Michigan. At least eight cities were being flooded by us. Dayton was pumping like an Iraq oil well, and I hadn't even started moving the work in bulk yet. The war had slowed up my progress with Elijah Slaughters, but it was still a work in progress. And once it was operating, Ohio was going to be our next spot to invade.

When Yahmo told me that, 'We're gonna get money when we get out,' I figured he meant he'd be able to get yay for the low low. But I had no idea that he was plugged like Pablo. The last shipment that arrived at Pets Warehouse in Hamtramck was 1,500 kilos.

Pets Warehouse sold all kinds of supplies, in bulk, for any and every pet imaginable. I had made a modest amount of investments that were very prosperous as well. My other legal ventures were also doing well. Live Lavish Realty being the most promising, but that was Tash' baby, and I was still unsure if I was going to ever deal with her, or it again.

Once my plane landed and I retrieved my luggage I rented a 2004 Taurus and headed to the hotel. When I checked in I was given a message, left by Yahmo, to meet him in the lounge at 8:00 p.m. That gave me about two hours to settle in and get something to eat before I hooked up with him.

When I walked into the lounge I spotted Yahmo at a back table enjoying the company of two cold females. I made my way toward the table, and as I approached he looked up and saw me.

"My man, what's really good?" He asked, as he stood up to shake my hand and greet me with a brotherly hug.

Smiling, I began to sit down, and said, "The sight of your company."

"I'm afraid their presence isn't everlasting. Unfortunately they won't be joining us for drinks or dinner," he said, as he dismissed them like they were common hood rats.

Once the women were gone we engaged in small talk until the waitress took our orders and returned with our drinks. "Tay, my, or Our Associates I should say have discovered what could become a big problem if we don't react immediately."

I tried not to look too concerned, but Yahmo's statement had me taken aback. "What kind of problem?" I asked.

"Well it seems that the Feds have been keeping a watchful eye on your cousin Jerome." When he said that, my stomach dropped, and I couldn't begin to mask the look of fear that I was sure my face was displaying. "It appears that they were told to keep an eye on him by someone named Eric Fleming. Do you know him?"

The name didn't ring a bell, so I just shook my head no.

"Well, he put Rome's name up for his bail about 6 months ago. They started watching him, but nothing turned up. So I guess they put more pressure on 'im, and he got them what they wanted."

"What choo mean? They got something on 'im?"

Yahmo started nodding his head. "Right now they got 'im wit' distributing 2 birds."

"What! I'll be damn! I know he ain't just sold nobody 2 slabs."

"I don't know," Yahmo said, "but I know that they aren't ready to indict him yet. Which means they're either trying to see what else he's into, or catch him up in a conspiracy. Either way the outcome could become worse than it is right now."

I found myself unable to speak. "Tay," I heard Yahmo call, bringing me back, "we need to do our own form of damage control."

"Meaning?"

"Meaning, Rome should turn himself in and cut a good, prearranged, deal."

"Dog it ain't no…"

Yahmo held up his hands to cut me off. And the look on his face displayed the seriousness of his next statement. "Tay, as your mans, I'm advising you to get Rome to do this. Not only will it stop a full fledge investigation, it'll be in the best interest of your organization."

My first instinct was to just blink out on Yahmo for what was an apparent threat. However, it was too early in the game for me to show my hand. Plus, what was being offered might actually be a better alternative.

I sat back in my chair, looked at Yahmo, and asked, "If he turns himself in and accepts his responsibility, how much time is he facing?"

Relieved that I was going to talk to Rome, Yahmo said, "I'm sure the Associates can ensure that his numbers are between 7 and 10 years."

****

As soon as I reached the city limits I called Rome and told him to meet me at Dibo's. Between 7 and 10 is good. Of course Rome wouldn't think so, but as the Don, it was my job to make him see the pros of the deal and disregard the cons. Had it been anyone else I could've just ordered them too, or had them eliminated.

I wanted Sig there, so I called him after I called Rome. They were both leaning against Sig's 89 Honda Accord smoking a blunt when I pulled into the parking lot. Once we went inside I got all three of us a beer and got right to it.

"Little brother you done phucked up!"

Him and Sig both looked at me like I was crazy. "Hold up, hold up. What's the problem Tay?" Sig asked, as Rome sat speechless.

I looked at Rome and began to tell him about the phucked up situation he was in. "Rome do you know a nigga named Eric Fleming?"

He dropped his head for a second, then looked back up at me. "Yeah," he said. "That was my man I used to phuck wit' while you was gone."

"Well he got knocked and offered you as a sacrificial lamb to the wolves. But if you wouldn't have sold him two thangs, having your name wouldn't have been shit."

With a look of disgust Rome said, "I ain't sell that bitch shit! He used to always get at me. So when he called me, on his knuckles, I gave him two to get on his feet."

"He got on his feet alright. Right now they can indict you for the distribution of two keys."

I went on to tell them about everything Yahmo had told me that could also lead to an indictment. As soon as I finished, Rome asked, "So now I gotta go on da run?"

"No, that's not a part of the plan," I said.

"Well what's the plan? You want me to fight it!"

"Nope. We'll have Pep check into this matter. If the charge is what I hear it is then you'll turn yourself in and take the deal that'll be offered."

"You must've been assured that a gravy deal would be put on the table," Sig said.

"I don't give a phuck what kinda deal is on the table. I ain't turning myself in to do a bit. Yall both must be crazy as hell!"

"Dig," I said, "you the one that done phucked up. If you don't take one for the team then the whole team could go down. Doing a bit is a part of this game we play. And getting good numbers is a victory in itself. It might be a small one, but it's a victory."

"How much time he looking at?"

"My man said between 7 and 10."

"Oh you gotta take that Rome!" Sig excitedly stated.

That's exactly why I wanted Sig there. He understood the importance of the numbers game. And he'd be able to help me persuade Rome.

"When will we know what's what?" Rome asked.

"I'll get Pep on top of it a-sap."

****

Every since I fell out with Tash I was either over one of my females cribs or staying in a suite at the Westin Hotel, downtown.

And since I had plans to hook-up with Shanice that night, I headed downtown as soon as I left Dibo's. I'd been looking forward to hollering at her since I met her the night that drama jumped off. But there were a couple of calls that I needed to make before playtime.

As soon as I got to the room I called Yahmo. I informed him that our lawyer would get on top of it as soon as he told me the lines of communication were open. He said he'd get on top of it, and I'd hear from him soon. After I hung up from talking to Yahmo, I called and left a message on Pep's answering machine to let him know to call me in the morning.

Chapter Twenty-Five

Tasha was in the kitchen washing dishes when the doorbell rang. She didn't really want to be bothered, but Tay had spent the night over one of his friends house, so ignoring the phone or the doorbell wasn't an option. She went to the door and looked out the peephole. She couldn't help but to smile at the sight of Trina hopping up and down.

"Girl, what's wrong wit' choo?" She asked, when she opened the door.

"Bitch I gotta pee," Trina answered, rushing past Tasha, "then we going to the hospital," she continued, as she dropped her coat and purse in the living room, and hurried toward the bathroom.

Tasha didn't know why they were going to the hospital, but she went into the kitchen and called Antoine's mother and told her to drop Tay at her parents' house. Then she called her mother and told her what little she did know, and that she'd call her from the hospital. As she was hanging up the phone Trina walked in the kitchen putting on her coat.

"Come on, get your coat and shit, and let's go."

"What we going to the hospital for?"

"Landa went into labor."

Tasha didn't utter a word. She went and threw on her shoes and a coat and they were out the door.

In the car Trina excitedly explained to Tasha what happened. "We were on the phone gossiping about your depressed ass." She looked over at Tasha and shook her head. "And the next thing I know, she yelled. Right before she yelled again I heard Rome ask her what was wrong. I couldn't understand what she said, but he picked up the phone and asked who it was. When I told him, he said its baby time and that he was taking her to Providence. So I told him I was gonna get choo, and we'd be on our way."

"It's about time. The baby was due two weeks ago. I thought it was gon' wait another week and be a turkey day baby."

When they arrived at the hospital the nurse at the front desk directed them to the maternity floor and they ran to the elevators. Ms. Madison was the first person they saw when they stepped off the elevator. She was pacing back and forth. When she saw Tasha and Trina, she hugged them both and said, "I can't believe my baby is about to be a mother."

Landa's nerdy little sister, Tiffany, was sitting down reading an American History book.

"Where's Rome?" Trina asked, after they all sat down.

"He's in there assisting the doctors," Ms. Madison said, smiling and pointing toward a set of double doors.

The women were engaging in small talk when the elevator bell sounded. A few seconds later Rome's mother entered the lobby. They all stood up and embraced her. As soon as they sat down the elevator bell rang again. Ms. Madison looked up and said, "This sure is a busy floor."

Rome's mother patted her on her knee, and said, "That's probably my ride."

When Tasha looked up and saw Tay she immediately stood up. It had been months since she'd last seen, or talked to him and he had a hard look to him. Her initial reaction was to run to him. But some hidden force cemented her feet to the floor, and she was unable to move. But before she knew it she had closed the distance between them and wrapped her arms around him. The hug she received in return wasn't as warm as the one she'd given, but she was grateful for it.

Tay spoke to everyone, then said he was going to the cafeteria to get something to drink. "Does anybody want anything?" he asked.

Everyone shook their head No, and he turned and headed toward the elevator. Tasha was deeply saddened, but when she turned around to sit down Rome's mother and Ms. Madison were gesturing for her to follow him, and she did.

They were both speechless on the elevator. The silence continued as they went thru the line an ordered their drinks. When they sat down, Tasha took a sip of her pink lemon-aid and looked across the table at Tay.

"You run out and get yourself hurt cause you're mad at me?" She asked, looking at the scar on the corner of his eye.

Instinctively, he reached up and touched it. "This didn't hurt nearly as bad as the pain you inflicted on me."

"Baby I am so sorry! Please understand that I didn't wanna tell you something that was gonna make you leave me.

"Well please understand that you shouldn't do shit that's gon' get choo left. How am I suppose to trust you now? I'm in and out of town all the time. And you've made it clear that when Missy needs to be scratched you're gonna get 'er scratched."

"That's not fair Tay, and you know it." What he said hurt, and upset her as well. "You love to get your dick sucked! So have you been true to me for the past three months?"

Tay remained calm and smiled. "This ain't about me," he said, "and don't question me. I ain't did nothin' fa you not to be able to trust me. And I definitely ain't put choo in no position to look like a damn fool."

Tears started racing down her face. "I know you haven't. And Baby I swear I'm sorry. I truly regret it. I just want choo to come home and let me be the partner to you that choo know I can be."

He put his hand on top of hers and just looked at her. She stared back at him, and the look in his eyes gave her a glimmer of hope. Not another word was spoken as they stood hand in hand and went back to the waiting room.

When Your Associates R More Dangerous Than U

Part 3

The Ends Justified The Means

...I miss 'im long as I'm livin' he's livin' thru
Memories he's there to kill all my suicidal
Tendencies in heaven lookin' over me or in hell
Keepin' it cozy I'm comin' life on these streets
Ain't what its 'spose ta be...

Jay-Z

Chapter Twenty-Six

The conclusion of another year was an evening away. 2003 had been wonderful, and with the exception of Rome's woes '04 was going to be even better. For Mary J. Blige, love was without a limit, but for **MCN,** work was without a limit. The only thing that remotely resembled a drought was the time that we would have to wait on the next shipment to arrive. After me and Tash' reconciliation I found it more difficult to fit Monique in. However, I was conducting more and more business in Ohio, and since Dayton was my base, she was still in the picture. And since I did love her, she lived like a mistress is supposed to.

I was in a position that most people think only takes place on TV. I could have easily left the game alone. But I wanted athlete money, and I wasn't phucking up my knees to get it. I had everything and was about to get more.

On Christmas Tash gave me a eight week old black pit bull puppy out of a Hound's Big Boy x Nardo's Tiny breeding. And I was as happy as Tay, when he looked underneath the tree, and it looked like

Toy's R Us. But she told me that I'd get my best gift in 8 more months.

All those thoughts had me smiling as I dried off. There was a big New Years Eve bash at the State Theater and me and my Queen were going to grace the Players and Playerettes with our presence.

****

The weather was terrible so we arrived in Tash' '03 gray Range Rover. The valet opened the door for Tash, and I tipped the lad a Grant when I rounded the truck. Although I am rather handsome, I was sure that the looks, from both males and females, were for my Angel. She looked like a little cub wrapped up in her full length Chinchilla with the hat and mittens to match. I was playing my matching Chinchilla, with the Chinchilla ball cap to the back for the thug appeal.

Inside, once we shed our furs, it was apparent that we were a notch, or two above all. Tash looked stunning in her black Ralph Lauren strapless dress and black full quill Ostrich heels. Around her neck rested my apology for hitting her; a classic riviere necklace. I'm sure every woman in the house wished that their neck was chilled by the diamond and platinum necklace set with 61GIA-certified round brilliant-cut natural diamonds. The center diamond was a 5.5 carat round brilliant, flanked by stones graduating to .5 at the clasp.

Since Tash was blinging enough for the both of us, I limited myself to the two carat solitaire diamonds in each ear, emerald cut diamond ring on my left pinkie and a Bulgari watch with the tan Italian leather band. I was decked out in a navy blue Ralph Lauren Purple Label suit, white Ralph Lauren shirt with a navy blue and tan Hermes' tie, and some tan Michael Anthony anteaters.

We were instantly greeted by MCN affiliates. It was definitely a night for the Ballers and their better halves. Me and Tash held hands as we made our way to the table that one of my Guys was leading us too. Surveying the scene, I saw quite a few of my associates throwing shots back and entertaining their dates. Trina and Tone were seated at the table, along with Que and Brenda when we walked up.

"My people my people. What's really good?" I said, as I pulled out a chair for Tash, and greeted the others at the surrounding tables. "Rome and Sig ain't made it yet, huh?"

Que pointed toward the dance floor. I looked and saw Rome and Landa cutting the rug. But what really surprised me was that Sig was on the floor with Keisha. He had been spending a lot of time with her, and he never brought a date to functions like that. "He must really dig her," I said.

Que looked toward the floor and smiled. "You know it's always one that tames you," he said, and put his arm around Brenda.

I tossed back a shot of Louis XIII and pulled Tash onto the floor. We were all on the floor having a ball. Before I knew it we were about 30 minutes away from the New Year. When we got back to the table the waiter furnished everybody with a glass of Cristal. I stood up and raised my glass.

"First of all I'd like to congratulate my lil brother and his lovely fiancée on the arrival of their month old son Jerome Jr. Bra, you deserve all that you're getting and will continue to get. I love you."

"I love you too dog."

"I'd also like to propose a toast to my man Sig, my dog Que and the rest of our family. Stay dedicated and loyal and we'll continue to get money longer than the Bush family.

"And last but surely not least," I said, looking at Tash, "I'd like to propose a toast to my better half. Tash you're the producer of the creations made from our love. You're my backbone as well as other things that don't lend themselves to conversational description, and I love you wit' all my heart."

"I love you too Baby," she responded, standing and giving me a short, but very meaningful kiss.

Everyone else stood as well, and we all drank up.

The rest of the night passed with no problems. And that was a helluva accomplishment! Rarely is there ever an event in Detroit that remains peaceful, especially a party that's full of liquor and ego's.

We began to clear out about 2:00 a.m. On the way out, Sig said that we needed to talk. Tonight. Even though the beef was over, I didn't want Tash out by herself that late, so I decided to take her. "Holla at Rome and we'll shoot up to my spot."

In the truck I cut the hazards on. "What we waiting on?" Tash asked.

"Gotta wait on Rome and Sig. We going to shoot up to Dibo's for a minute."

"Ahh Baby! I'm buzzing, horny and I want some of this." She reached over and started massaging my manhood thru my pants.

I looked in the rearview mirror and saw Rome's burgundy Denali sitting behind us. Then Sig pulled up next to me in his white Navigator and signaled that he was ready to roll.

"How long we gon' be there?" Tash asked, as we drove off.

"Not long. I just need to blow at them for a minute." I reached over and started fondling her breast and said, "You know I ain't gon' be long. I'm ready ta get choo home and break you off."

By the time we pulled into the parking lot, Tash was out like a light. "Tash," I said, tapping her leg.

"Hmm?"

"Come on Boo."

Tash, Landa and Brenda were all sleep on their feet as we walked into the club. Once inside I locked the door. Tash was behind the bar in the mini refrigerator pulling shit out as I headed toward my office.

"Yall want something to eat?" I heard her ask Landa and Brenda before I shut the door.

Sig was firing up a blunt when I walked in. I grabbed three Corona's out of my fridge and handed them one. Sig hit the trees a few times and passed the blunt to Rome.

"Dig," he said, "I found out some shit about that nigga Alex."

The mention of that name caught the attention of mine, that might've been elsewhere. I raised my eyebrows, but said nothing. Rome knew the name had taken me aback and passed me the blunt.

"It appears," Sig continued, "that he's doing some thangs. He got that boy! And not a bird or two. When I say he got that boy, I mean he got that boy."

"Damn. He doin' 'um like that?" Rome asked.

Sig looked at him and said, "Dog, he owns a steel company."

"What made you start inquiring about him?" I asked.

"Actually he was the one inquiring about you." I gave Sig a confusing look. "Yeah, my man Derrik told me some dude named Chips was asking about you. That dude was showing a lot of interest in you and your business. Dee said he didn't know why ole boy was being so nosey, but he knows you my mans, so he put me up on it. That's when I started trying to find out who Chips was. It turns out that its him."

Sig grabbed the blunt from Rome, hit it a couple of times and continued. "From what I hear, he used to only phuck wit' the boy, but then he started phuckin' wit' yay too.

"Remember I told you that Bo and them stopped phuckin' wit' me, but they was on like a muthatphucka?"

I started nodding my head. A picture began to form in my head, and I didn't like what I was seeing. "This shit is about Tash! That hoe ass nigga is the head man of the GN's. And that body is still functioning, cause we didn't decapitate them. We just left 'em wit' a weak pulse, and that's why we thought the beef was done. But he's got it simmering while he recoups."

We were all speechless. I had a smirk on my face, but it wasn't shit funny. Shit was about to be on the flo' again, but we had the advantage.

"Well it looks like it's about ta be on again." I said. "I'm high as hell right now and can't think strait. We'll get together tomorrow and discuss what we'll do. But you can believe it's about to be some fireworks in '04'."

Sig stood up and I gave him a play. He pulled me to him and hugged me. When he released me and stepped back, he said, "Tay this can't be personal dog. He made it personal and look at the way his mistakes are gon' cost him."

"I feel you. Always business. Never personal." I said, but how could it not be.

On the ride home I continuously looked over at Tash as she slept. My feelings changed with each glance. One moment I hated her, cause of all the pain and turmoil she caused. And the next minute I loved her, because of everything she is, and has been to us. Finally, I just stopped looking at her and turned the radio up.

As I drove my head filled with all kind of thoughts. First, I wondered how many cats she slept with. Then, I wondered what she did to this nigga Alex to make him want to beef with me, about my HOE! The thoughts were unbearable, and I was happy to be pulling into the garage.

Tara greeted us at the door. Tash headed for the stairs, and I let Tara out. While Tara ran around in front of the house I call Monique to tell her Happy New Year. We talked for about 15 minutes. I assured her that I'd be down there by the end of the month. Then I whistled for Tara, and went in the house.

When I walked in the bedroom the lights were out. I touched my bedside lamp and the dim light came on. Tash was in the bed, and looked like she was into her second dream. The light on the answering machine blinking was, so I hit play.

There were a few messages from people calling to say Happy New Year. Rome called to say, "Dog we made it home. Holla at cha tomorrow. Love you."

Then I heard Pep's voice. "Mr. Manning this is Mr. Peppers. I have some disturbing news. Please call me first thing in the morning."

Chapter Twenty-Seven

"I wonder what kinda bomb Pep is about to drop on us."

"I haven't the slightest idea," I told Rome, as we headed out to Bloomfield Hills.

After hearing the message that Pep had left on my answering machine I became nervous. I laid awake all night wondering what the problem was. Figuring that the news was going to dampen Rome's spirits, I waited until after I talked to Pep and arranged to meet him at his house before I called and informed Rome of his message.

Rome stared out the window in silence as we rode. My thoughts were focused on what we would do if the deal fell thru, like I was figuring it had. Not only wouldn't Rome accept a boatload of time, I wouldn't want him too.

"Well Road Dog, lets see what's poppin'," I said, pulling into Peps driveway.

"Pep sure is doing well," Rome said, looking at the house as we walked up the walkway.

"He's always made a nice livin', but once we got on, his salary began to mirror a sports agent. Then he moved out here about a year ago," I said, approaching the front door, and ringing the doorbell.

Peps wife answered the door and smiled when she saw me. "Dontae, how are you doing? I haven't seen you in awhile. Come on in."

"I'm alright Mrs. Peppers. How've you been?"

"Besides the arthritis in my hands I'm doing fine."

"That's good. This is my brother Jerome. Rome this is Mrs. Peppers." They shook hands and she led us down a long hall to a room that was obviously Pep's home office.

When we walked in, Mrs. Peppers turned around and left, closing the door behind her. Pep looked up from his paperwork and took off his glasses as me and Rome took seats in the two leather chairs in front of his desk.

"First of all," he began, "the deal won't be as good as you want. And, I also found out that a Quincy Lomas is being investigated." Me and Rome looked at each other with a mixture of shock and fear. "I'm still trying to find out what prompted the investigation, and what kind of case they're trying to build."

"I thought the deal was gonna be sweet. What happened?" I asked.

"Well, when I first contacted the man you told me to call, we talked briefly and he told me he'd call me back. When he called me back he said the deal was a no go."

"Why?"

"He said they're informant was willing to stretch his truths in order to be granted immunity for the charges he's facing. But he said they're offering 15 ye…"

"PHUCK THAT!" Rome angrily stated, standing up. "Ain't no way in hell I'm willingly gon' take no damn 15 years!" Rome threw his hands up in the air and said, "Pep, you just phucked up my whole day wit' that statement."

"I can only imagine. But I'm not surprised that they reneged on the deal. They get the informants to do their dirty work, then they push it to the limit."

"Well without the rat they don't have nothing," I said.

Pep looked at me and said, "I know what you're getting at, but his statements are already on file. And if he... How can I say this? If he's unavailable when they need him then they probably will make things hard for you all."

"Can you get this shit put off for awhile?"

"Tay that's no problem. That's why I make the big bucks," he said, smiling at me. "Just be extra careful. Don't give them anymore ammunition." We nodded our heads, shook Pep's hand and left.

Rome was quiet the entire ride home. My thoughts were racing as well. We were both in such deep thought that when I pulled into his driveway, I killed the engine and we both just stared out the window.

After a few minutes, Rome looked at me. He broke the silence by asking me, "What choo gon' do 'bout Que?"

"I haven't decided yet. Que's a stand up dude, but I've seen them people break a lot of cats. I don't know if I wanna wait and let this shit get too far out of control. I'm a just take a few days to think it thru. But I'm more worried about your situation."

"Oh! We ain't gon' worry about that. I got about 8 million in my account in Belize, and a few mil here and there in other various accounts. I'm a start getting shit in order, cause I ain't doin' no bit. And when it's time to roll I'll be ready."

"I know my peoples gon' be mad that choo ain't taking the deal, but phuck 'em! I'll let 'em know that things didn't turn out like we wanted, and that we'll deal accordingly."

"Man this year ain't two days old and its already phucked up. Me and Landa get married in June, and I ain't told 'er what's goin' on."

"Whew! L.L. got choo phucked up."

"L.L.?"

"Love and Landa. Nigga, you don't tell 'er shit! Yall gon' get married, and if there's a problem we'll leave the states for awhile. In the meantime be careful like Pep said, and enjoy yourself. I'm a go home go to sleep and figure out what we gon' do 'bout Alex' hoe ass. Dude outta there!"

Rome had a silly smirk on his face and said, "Sig's info done really gave you a reason to put dudes head ta bed."

"Shut up and get outta my car," I said, laughing.

I left Rome's and headed home. Ironically, Jay-Z's '**It Was All Good Just A Week Ago**' was playing as I drove to the crib. I called Que and told him to meet me at Dibo's at 10:00 p.m. Then I called and told Yahmo to meet me in Sin City in two days.

When I got home I went in the living room and crashed on the couch. It seemed like I had just fallen asleep when Tash woke me up and told me that Sig was there to see me. I looked at my watch and saw that I had been sleep for almost 5 hours. It was damn near 6 o'clock. "Where he at?" I asked.

"In the kitchen."

I went and brushed my teeth, then joined Sig in the kitchen. He was at the table eating some Fruit Loops when I walked in. "What's up muthaphucka?"

He ate a spoonful of cereal and said, "Ain't shit poppin'. I stopped by to see what's up wit' this Alex shit. It's apparent that at some point dude is gon' try to have you hit. I think we should snatch that bitch ass nigga up and make life miserable fa 'im."

"I agree wit' choo. I ain't acquired too much prestige to where I won't get my hands bloody. But I'm goin' out of town the day after tomorrow. As soon as I get back its on."

"Well I'll have everythang in place when you get back. All we'll have to do is go pick 'im up."

"Bet. We'll push it to his bitch ass like we did dude in da joint. But dig this, the deal didn't go thru fa Rome. They talking 'bout 15 now."

"You bullshittin'!"

"Hell naw. I wish I was. And not only that. Que's ass is under investigation too."

"All man. That's phucked up. We gon' put 'im in the trunk too?"

"I don't know dog. I'm a think 'bout it while I'm gone. I don't want too. Pep is gon' find out what they trying ta do to 'im."

Sig put his bowl in the sink, turned around and said, "Make sure you don't allow your personal feelings to affect your decision. We both would like to think that Que can handle the pressure, but we also know how them people break cats. And truthfully, I think they know 'bout us."

I looked at Sig in disbelief. "Fa real?" I asked.

"Tay, you ain't no fool. Think about it. We was both heavy in the game before we ever caught a case. And not too long after you come home we was right back in the thick of it. It's just that we've been shrewd in our moves, but they'll be at us the first break they get. Think about that dog."

I remained silent and in deep thought. Sig put on his coat, gave me a play and left. I went in the backyard with the intentions of feeding my dogs and giving Screwface a shot of penicillin, but ended up staying out there for damn near two hours. I put Roxie on the treadmill and let her work the spring pole for awhile before I went in to take a shower. Once I got out of the shower I threw on a pair of S.

Carter blue jeans, a orange S. Carter sweatshirt and my blue alligator cowboy boots with the gold studs. I played a couple of games of chess on my computer to pass time, then headed to Dibo's.

On the ride to my club I thought about the disaster that could take place if Que was indicted, and didn't stand strong. He, more so than anyone, could put me away for life. And I needed to decide whether or not I trusted him enough to let the hand that's being dealt play out. Or if I needed to intervene and cheat while the cards were still being shuffled.

Que was at the bar talking to Marcel when I walked in. When he seen me he got up and followed me to my office. I gave Marcel the peace sign and told him to let me know if Shanice called.

"What's really good my man?" Que asked, shutting the door.

"Ain't shit. Just needed to holla at choo 'bout a few thangs."

"What's up?"

"Have you been feeling like everythang is perfect and we ain't got no problems?"

"Pretty much. These hoe ass beefs we been in don't make me lose no sleep."

"Me either. It ain't like we beefin' wit' muthaphuckas that we can't beat. But I been thinking 'bout problems that're gon' come in the future and hit us wit' a heavy blow."

"Like what?"

"Like the Feds. Shit seems too good to be true right now, and I'm thinking 'bout chillin' for awhile."

Que started nodding his head slowly and looked at me. "Sometimes I be thinking 'bout that too," he began. "We done had a good run, and I'd hate to get knocked and not be able to enjoy life. I've already got more money than I ever thought I'd have.

"When you gon' pump the brakes? After the next shipment?"

Shaking my head, I said, "Naw. I've already pumped 'em. I just needed to holla at my main man and see if my way of thinking had gotten soft."

"That way of thinking ain't soft. It's being smart."

"Glad to hear you say that. That's all I wanted to holla at choo about," I said, standing up. "And too let choo know that operation is down for now."

"Aiight. Well I'm out. I'll hit choo later and see what's up."

As soon as Que left I called Pep and left a message on his machine for him to get on top of Que's investigation. And just as I kicked back and fired up a blunt Marcel buzzed me and told me that Shanice was on line two. I took a couple of hits from the blunt and pressed the blinking light.

"My chocolate delight, what's goin' on?"

"That's whut me should be askin' you, since me don't hear from you now dat cha back home wit' girlfriend. Me really surprised that choo called."

"Girlfriend is not all that's been keeping me busy. But enough of the idle chatter, I called to extend an invitation to you."

"Well talk ta me Rude Boy. You know me like when you no beat 'round the bush."

Her words made me smile. The sound of her voice was a loin waker. That Jamaican accent drove me crazy. And the things she did to me while she talked that shit had me addicted. "How 'bout we go to Vegas and do a lil sinning in Sin City? Then head to Hawaii for a few days?"

"Only if you help me into a club that me been wontin' ta join."

Taken aback, I curiously asked her, "What club?"

"The Mile High Club!"

"No problem," I said. "I'll pick you up in the morning. And you don't need to pack anything. We'll acquire essentials as needed."

****

When we arrived at the MGM Grand the valet opened my door. "What's up Mr. Manning? Your suite is ready."

"Thanks Jeff. We don't have any bags, but I'll be back down in about 30 minutes," I said, as I passed him a Grant.

"The car will be here. And if you check under your pillow you'll like the gift I brought back from Portland."

"My man." I got my key card from the front desk and we headed up to the room.

"This is beautiful," Shanice said, looking around when we stepped inside the suite.

"Go in the bedroom and look under the pillows. You should find something to your likin'."

She headed toward the bedroom and I grabbed a seat on the couch in the living room area so I could call Yahmo. I told him I had arrived a day early. He told me that he'd fly out tomorrow afternoon and we could hook up tomorrow evening.

I looked over at Shanice when I hung up the phone and smiled. "You like?" I asked, watching her cut up the buds with scissors.

"Hell yeah me like! This is real ganja," she said, picking up the buds and rolling it between her thumb and index finger.

I picked up the bag of weed and admired it. It was about six stalks of some of the prettiest weed I'd ever seen. The crystals were shining like diamonds in the sun, and it was purple.

"How 'bout we shoot downstairs and hit the tables after we smoke? Then we'll go to the show at the Mirage. Ashanti is performing."

She straddled me and put a perfectly rolled blunt between my lips. Looking me in my eyes as she lit the blunt she said, "Rude Boy, whateva you wanna do wit', or too me, I'm down for." Then she lifted up my shirt and started kissing on my chest and stomach. Easing off my lap she got on her knees between my legs and began to unbuckle my belt. "I love being in your presence and wanna get choo away from girlfriend," she continued, looking up at me, piercing me with those green eyes.

Before I knew it I felt her warm mouth engulf all 10 inches of my manhood. I gave a light gasp as I took a long pull off the blunt. Laying my head back holding my breath I savored the taste of the weed while experiencing a drug induced and sexual high.

At some point the feeling became so exhilarating that I was unsure if I was intoxicated from the weed, or the head. I looked down at Shanice in amazement and watched her perform an act that could only be described as unbelievable. Before I knew it I was in a euphoric state, feeling like my soul was being sucked from me as I exploded in her mouth. And she didn't let up.

Needless to say, we never left the room. That episode led to a night of wild, untamed fucking all over the room.

****

Me and Shanice were at the mall shopping when Yahmo called me. He told me to meet him at The Mirage in two hours. We dipped into Victoria's Secret for a 'Buy the sluttiest shit' spree, and hit a few more stores before we left.

Yahmo was in the lounge at the bar having a drink when we walked in. I introduced him to Shanice, tossed her a inch stack and told her to go have some fun, but be back in an hour. Hopefully me and Yahmo would be finish talking and we could be on our way to Hawaii.

"Damn you keep good company," he said, giving me a hug. Then we both watched her strut away.

We went and sat at a table in the back. Even though it was only 2:00 p.m. the lounge was a little less than full. I ordered a Margarita, heavy on the Quevo, then we sat down.

Once the waiter brought my drink and left, Yahmo looked at me and asked, " So what's the deal Playboy? Is everythang everythang?"

"Hell naw!" I told him. "They ain't talkin no less than 15. And we'd rather take our chances wit' 12 in da box." I didn't tell 'im that if shit wasn't right we was gon' get ghost.

"Tay the Associates ain't gon' like this decision. We agreed that whateva the deal was that he'd take it."

"No! We agreed that he'd take between 7 and 10. Yahmo, the number is too high dog. I ain't telling my brother ta go lay down fa no 15 years."

"Tay the stakes are high too. If they don't feel safe shit can dry up like the Sahara in June."

The last thing I wanted to do was lose my plug. But I didn't wanna lose my brother for 15 years either. And if I had to choose… Phuck the plug! But Lord knows that I didn't wanna lose it. "Look. At some point the kind of money we gettin' has got to get better than decade and a half numbers. Shid! Wit' the latest deal we'll be making yall over 100 million a year! Hell, if I had the resources, a nigga making that kinda money wouldn't do a day, let alone years."

"Tay, this shit is much bigger than us dog. You ain't the only one generating doh, and you and your people ain't the only ones expected to take the deals that are on the table. But what I will do is call and see why it turned out like it did."

"My man," I said, standing up. "Call me as soon as you hear something."

We gave each other a play and a brotherly embrace, and I headed out to find my stallion. My phone started vibrating as I was walking thru the casino. As soon as I answered, Tash rambled off some of the worse news that I could receive.

I had Shanice paged, and waited impatiently. The 10 minutes it took for her to show up seemed like forever. She approached me with a big smile on her face, and two floor men in tow, with a couple of racks of chips.

"Baby me luck has..."

I grabbed her hand and said, "C'mon we gotta go! Follow me," I told the floor man, and headed toward the exit.

I was scouring the joint as we walked until I saw what I was looking for. Approaching two elderly ladies sitting at the slot machines. I told the floor men, "Give these lovely ladies a tray a piece."

They both stood up and said, "Thank you young man," while hugging me.

"You're very welcome. That's a little somethin' to help wit' them grandbabies college tuition," I told them, and gave them both a kiss on the cheek.

On the ride back to the hotel I gained a lot of respect for Shanice. From the time I told her to come on she just did as I asked, and didn't ask any questions. "When we get to the room we gon' grab our stuff and head to the airport. I gotta get home, but I owe you a trip."

She reached over and grabbed my hand, and said, "Okay."

My phone started ringing as I gathered my things. The last time I answered I was given terrible news, so I wanted to let it ring, but I couldn't do that. "Yeah," I said, when I answered.

"Tay you passported up?" Yahmo asked.

"Yeah. Why?"

"Cause we leave for Ecuador in the morning. The Associates wanna meet wit' choo, so cancel you and girlies plans."

"Naw. Cancel the trip. I gotta get home! One of my mans done got killed, and anotha one is in critical."

"Look, as soon as you get shit in order, hit me. This meeting must take place. And the sooner the better."

Chapter Twenty-Eight

Tasha couldn't believe her ears. On her way back into the kitchen she overheard Tay and Sig talking about Alex. 'That muthaphucka wants my man dead,' she thought. 'Ain't no way in hell I'd be able to live with myself.' She went back upstairs and as soon as she heard Tay leave she called Landa.

"Girl, you know that muthaphucka Alex wants to kill Tay!" She said, as soon as Landa answered the phone.

"What! How you figure that?"

" Today I heard Tay and Sig talking about it. Chips must be crazy if he thinks I'm a let him kill my man.

"Tasha, you saying that like you gon' stop 'im."

"Shid! I am."

"What! Tasha. Girl look. You know if their up on his ass then their gonna handle it."

Tasha broke down crying. Her conscious was really eating away at her. She felt like she was the cause of it because she had been involved with Alex.

"Landa you don't understand. When Chips ass wants something done it gets done. I know Tay ain't no pushover, but Alex associates wit' some powerful people."

"So what are you gon' do?

" I don't know yet. But he ain't killing my man. I'm about to sit here and think about something. And when I do I'll call you."

"Okay."

Her mind was racing as she thought of the possibility of losing Tay. Her first thought was that she'd get Alex somewhere and kill him, but she shook that idea. She knew that she'd have to be face to face with danger in order to take a life. True enough, danger was around the corner, but it wasn't in her face, so she started thinking of something else.

Knowing that Tay hadn't made any moves she figured that the fight hadn't actually started. Meaning Alex might not be aware of Tay's knowledge of his wanting him killed. So that would mean that she didn't know either, and she might be able to prevent anything from happening.

Tasha grabbed some clothes, some lingerie and her make-up bag and packed it in her Gucci overnight bag. She called Lil Tay in the house and had him pack an overnight bag as well. She dropped him off over her parents house and headed out to the Ritz Carlton in Dearborn. Once she checked in she took a hot bath then laid down and went to sleep.

She must have been tired cause not only did she sleep thru the night, she didn't awake until almost noon. After brushing her teeth and washing her face she called Alex.

"Hello."

"What's up stranger?" She said, at the sound of the deep voice that used to get her juices flowing.

Tasha could hear in his voice that not only was he surprised, but also happy to hear from her by the way he said, "Mini Me! Long time no hear from. What's up? I thought it'd be a while before I heard from you."

"Well, I was kinda enjoying the way that you were coming at me. Then my healthy ego was dealt a helluva blow when the pursuit stopped, so I figured I'd go on offense."

"Don't think you haven't been thought of. I was just biding my time. Ole boy seems to have your undivided attention."

"Mine and every other tramp he's sticking his dick in."

"Uh-oh. Is there trouble in paradise?"

"Naw. Not really. But if he can have fun I plan too."

"Is that why you're at the Ritz Carlton? Having fun." Caller I.D. was a bitch she thought to herself. She didn't want any flags to be raised, so she had to think fast. "No. I still have morals and standards. I came here the other day after I left Fairlane Shopping Mall. After we got into it, about one of his hoes calling the house, I went shopping, and rather than go home, I just got a room."

"Well, you know I'm dying to see you."

With a southern drawl, Tasha said, "Why Chips, are you pursuing lil ole me?"

"If you're not going back on defense, then I'm in hot pursuit."

"Whatever you say Mr. Bryant. We playing by your rules now."

"In that case, tomorrow we'll kick it off. I got a lot of business to take care of today, but I won't disappoint you with what I'll have planned for us tomorrow."

"Think I don't know that? Just call and fill me in on what, where and when. We'll take care of the how together."

"Fa sho'."

She gave him her cell number and hung up the phone. Tasha laid back unknowing of what she was gonna do, but she had put her plan in motion…Whatever it is.

If she was gonna use her powers of persuasion in an intimate way to extract any kind of info from Alex then she had to look good. Tasha called Jason and was happy that he had an opening.

During the ride to the shop she thought about the task that was before her. Even though she hated to admit it, sleeping with Alex wasn't the part of her mysterious plan that she was dreading. She knew he'd never tell her exactly what his plans were, but what she did know was that he had a real weakness for her. If she displayed enough distaste for Tay and their relationship he'd give her an inclination of how much he disliked Tay, and if he planned to do something to him. After he did she'd tell Tay that she overheard him and Sig talking and went out with Alex to get info outta him. Of course she'd omit the part about them having sex, but she hoped Tay wouldn't be real mad, and he'd allow her to help him eradicate the problem.

The following evening Tasha smoked a blunt as she relaxed in her bubble bath. Usually she only smoked with Tay, but she needed to smoke tonight cause she was so unsure of what she was gonna do. As the steam intensified her high, she became paranoid, and started having second thoughts about smoking, seeing Alex, and everything else that came to mind.

Tasha was dosing off when the phone rang. Luckily Alex called to let her know that he was on his way, or she may have slept until she either drowned, or the water turned cold. After she hung up the phone she brushed her teeth and proceeded to get dressed.

Alex arrived about an hour and a half later. When Tasha opened the door she was in awe of the man that she still cared about. Underneath his full length bear coat, he was decked out in an olive green Gianni Campagna suit with 14 carat gold pinstripes, olive green and gold two toned Mediterranean turtle shoes and a 3 carat solitaire diamond in his left ear. Alex not only looked good to her, he looked as powerful as any president that's been inaugurated.

He too was inebriated at the sight of Tasha standing before him in a gold Vera Wang dress that exposed ribs on the right side, and barely covered all of her thighs. Her gold Jimmy Choo's gave her a little height. She still had to raise up on her tippy-toes when she greeted him with a light, but 'yeah you getting some' kiss on the lips.

"Wow!" He said. "You look stunning. And I am really impressed, cause I didn't think you could look better in person than you do in my dreams."

Tasha raised her right arm and struck a pose. "Compliments will only get choo seconds," she said, as she turned around allowing him a view of the whole package. "Let me get my coat and we can be on our way."

She donned her full length white sable, but didn't wanna mess up her hair, so she left the hat, and they left.

Waiting in front of the hotel when they walked out was a gray Rolls Royce Phantom. The driver opened and closed the door for them, got in and they left.

"This is beautiful," Tasha said, looking around.

Alex released a light chuckle and said, "Mini Me, this and anything else you want is yours." Taking her hand in his, he continued, "Just be wit' me. Let me love you, and take care of you."

Tasha leaned her head on his shoulder and told him, "Leaving Tay won't be that easy. He'll try to prevent me from being with you."

He wrapped his arm around her and said, "Don't worry." They rode listening to jazz, both in deep thought about the same man.

They arrived at Sea For Yourself, a seafood restaurant in Bloomfield Hills. Tasha was impressed that Alex remembered that she was a seafood lover. The maitre d' greeted Alex like he was a regular, then escorted them to their table. He handed them two menus as he asked if they would like something to drink.

"White wine for the lady," Alex said, pointing toward Tasha, "and a Brandy for me. We'll be ready to order in a minute."

Tasha admiringly glanced at Alex and asked him, "What kept you from me yesterday?"

"I had to try and get some things done, but I keep running into a roadblock, and it's frustrating. But tonight, and hopefully the rest of our lives, I'm all yours."

"Let's just enjoy the here and now. True enough, I am getting fed up with Tay's whorish ways, but I don't know if I'm strong enough to just up and leave him. Plus, being wit' choo might be the same. Yall men with power think you can do anything you want too."

"Tasha, ole boy might have a little clout in the streets, and is adjusting to his new found fanfare. I, on the other hand, have always had power, so it won't affect my behavior. I have money, and I'm very successful, and above all, I know how to handle it."

Their food arrived, and they made small talk while they ate. The meal was delicious and by the time they were ready to leave, Tasha was a little tipsy. The four glasses of wine had definitely balanced out the high that she had from earlier. She was no longer in such a mellow mood. Now she was feeling real frisky and looking forward to getting back to her room with Alex.

A little voice inside her kept telling her that its only business. But she knew in her heart that what that voice was saying was Bullshit!

On their way back to her hotel room Tasha received a call from Trina. She was tempted to turn her phone off, and call her back in the morning, but she noticed that Trina had been constantly calling all night.

"What's up girl?" Tasha said, when she answered her phone. Trina was so hysterical that Tasha couldn't understand what she was saying. "Trina. Slow down. I can't understand you. What's wrong?"

"Tasha, he's gone!" She said crying.

Tasha's heart started beating real fast and she became real nervous. "Who? Gone where?" She asked.

"Tone! They killed him! They killed 'im Tasha!"

"I'm on my way." Tasha turned to look at Alex and told him, "I need you to take me to Trina's."

Chapter Twenty-Nine

When we landed at Metro, I rented a car, and for the first time, I got the Cadillac for its power under the hood, and not for its looks. God was definitely riding with me, cause I whipped up in front of Sinai Hospital in about 25 minutes and didn't get pulled over by the Police.

"Take the car, and I'll holla at choo later," I told Shanice, then hurried inside.

After I got the necessary info I took the elevator to the 6th floor. When I walked into room 1660 my stomach dropped. Sig had tubes in his nose and I.V.'s in his arms, and the whole left side of his face was swollen. If Keisha hadn't been sitting there holding his hand I might've thought that I was in the wrong room.

I gently tapped Keisha on the shoulder to wake her up. "What happened?" I asked, staring at Sig.

"I don't know, exactly. Ms. Langford called me yesterday and told me that he got shot. I've been here every since. Ms. Langford was so out of it that the doctor gave her some sleeping pills. Your brother just left about a half hour ago to take her home."

"What are they saying about his condition?" I asked, pointing at Sig.

"Right now it's not looking too good. He got shot 3 times in the chest, and once in the face. They don't know when he's gonna come outta his coma."

"What he get hit wit'?"

"I think I heard 'um say a 9 millimeter."

I went down to the lobby to call and let Tash know I was back in town. "What's up Love," I said, when I heard her voice.

"Nothing much. Where you at?"

"At the hospital wit' Sig. I came here strait from the airport. Where you at?"

"Me and Landa are here wit' Trina. Baby, she's a mess. She'll sleep for about 20 minutes and then she'll just wake up screaming."

"Look. Get in touch wit' Tone's sister, Rachael, and find out where they want the funeral held. Then let her know you'll take care of all the arrangements if they're not up to it. And call Rome and tell him to come get me from here."

"Okay Baby. I love you, and be careful."

"I will, and I love you too."

I went back up to Sig's floor and was able to talk to one of his doctors. I found out that two of the shots had cracked his chest plate, and the third was an inch away from his heart. The odds of him waking up were 60/40 against him. And if he did wake up, the doctor said it'd take several surgeries to even begin to fix his face. All in all, someone had killed my dog and phucked my mans up.

Rome woke me up a couple of hours after I had nodded out on the empty bed in Sig's room. I told Keisha to call me if there was a change in Sig's condition and that I'd be back tomorrow. On the way out I called my lil dog Ty and told him to bring Keisha some food up to the hospital.

"Shoot ta my crib," I told Rome, when we got in the car.

"Aiight. Where was you at yesterday? I called you a million times afta I found out what happened."

"Man I turned my phone off. I was freakin' wit' dat bitch Shanice and didn't wanna be interrupted. I'm a have ta stop doin' that."

Rome looked over at me and said, "Hell yeah you are! Especially when one of us is out of town."

"You're right," I agreed. "Have you been able to find out anything?" I asked.

"Nothing concrete."

"So this was probably a hit," I said, more so to myself than to Rome.

Although, we had shut down a lot of cats operations, and the hit could have come from a number of people, I knew that Alex had to be behind this one. We've had quite a few soldiers fall over the last couple of years, but besides Lil Tee, this was the closest hit to home I'd experienced. I was really feeling it. I kept hearing Sig's voice resonating in my head. "Tay you can't take this personal baby! Plan. Plan your next move," it kept saying. Lord knows that I wanted to ignore those words and go kill Alex. But just like he is, most of the time, in the flesh, Sig was right in the spiritual form as well.

When we got to my crib I told Rome, "Get Junior, Keith, and a few other cats, and meet me at Dibo's later on tonight. I gotta go in and lay down for awhile."

"Aiight dog. Love you."

"Love you too."

****

Tone's funeral was held at Greater Grace Temple. It was jam packed. Of course MCN was there, but a lot of our associates were there as well.

Due to the damage to his face and head the casket had to remain closed. Whether it was from having already lost two sons, or just being the typical strong single black woman that she is, Ms. Thompson held up well. Rachel and Tone's younger brother Kyle was a mess. I'm sure Trina's conscious was eating away at her, as was Kyle's. He stayed mad at Tone because Tone was so tough on him about school and hanging out.

Unlike a lot of black males, Tone was known by the pastor that conducted the service, so his speaking was real and from the heart. I read the obituary, and as I went thru it, I became teary eyed. On the front was a picture of Tone in black Sean John jeans, a gold and black Gucci shirt with a pair of gold and black gator cowboy boots and his gold mink. Throughout the obituary were colorful pictures of Tone with Trina and other members of his family. On The back was a picture of me, Tone, Sig, and Rome suited and booted at a party Puff had in Miami.

After the funeral I joined everyone at Ms. Thompson's for a while. I knew that Tasha wanted to look after Trina so I told her to call me when she wanted to meet me at home, then I headed to the hospital to check on my mans.

****

Over the next couple of months I went to see Sig on a daily basis, but his condition remained the same. Business continued to boom, and I put people in position to pick up the void left by Sig. I started dealing with even more people than I wanted too, cause I didn't trust any one person other than Sig and Rome to mash 3 and 4 hundred bricks on at a time. Monique's brother, Brian, turned out to be a real money getter, but until I was able to get down there for an extended period of time he was getting no more 50 at a time. Elijah Slaughters was running well, but I was anxious to put it to use.

Trina was still stressing, so I used it to my advantage. I treated her and Tasha to a two week vacation in Cancun. Landa wasn't ready to be away from Rome Jr., so she didn't accompany them.

After I took Tash and Trina to the airport I dropped Tay off at Mr. and Mrs. Foster's house. Then I went to the grocery store and bought some things for the house I'd bought in the suburbs last week. And since I had a few hours to spare before I headed back out to Metro, I went to see my mans.

Keisha and Ms. Langford were at Sig's bedside when I walked in the room. Ms. Langford greeted me with a hug and a kiss, and told me that nothing had changed. I told them that I'd sit with him for a couple of hours, and they could go home and rest. They both accepted my invitation to relieve them, and left.

Sig's hair and beard had grown like wild weeds. It wasn't unkept, but it could stand to be trimmed up. The other day I had noticed that the swelling in his face was down, so I took my trimmers with me that day.

"Well Road Dog, you laying up in this bitch like we don't need you," I said, as I put the guard on the trimmers and proceeded to cut his hair. "Nigga you gotta wake da phuck up. I ain't made no moves on that hoe ass nigga yet. Business was getting sloppy, and since you wanna cat nap I gotta focus on that. I was suppose to been had a meeting wit' da heavyweights, but I told Yahmo I'd hit 'im when your status upgraded. I'm sure they're appalled, but they ain't tripping. Them girls still come every month."

Once I finished cutting his hair I began to line him up. "I gotta go get Monique from the airport at 5:30," I continued.

"I was missing my baby, so she's coming up here to spend a couple of weeks wit' me. Tash and Trina will be in Cancun. I bought a crib in Southfield and plushed it out for us. You know I ain't no disrespectful dude. Can't have her up in wifee's spot. Hell, Keisha has been right by your side since you've been here. When you wake up you're going to have to bling 'er down."

I buzzed the nurse to come give Sig a sponge bath and change his sheets. "You look like a new man," I said, brushing the excess hair off him. "When you wake up we'll go to Brazil and get their best doc to fix your face."

When the nurse came in I looked at her name tag and said, "Nurse Krystal, would you please bathe my mans and change his bed linen?"

"The woman that's here everyday told me to make sure our male orderlies do that," she said, hunching her shoulders and smiling.

I couldn't do nothing but laugh. Keisha had staked her claim and was serious. I couldn't wait to tell Sig that. "Well she won't be back no time soon," I told her. Reaching in my pocket, I continued, "I'd appreciate it if you did it," I told her, and gave her a Benjamin.

"You don't have to pay me."

"I know, but he'd be really offended if you weren't tipped."

"Thank you," she said, accepting the money. "I'll go get the stuff."

I looked at Sig with my arms spread and said, "See how ya mans lookout fa you!"

****

Monique looked scrumptious when she got off the plane. We engaged in a kiss full of such passion that people began to stare. I pulled away and just looked at her from head to toe. "Damn I've missed you. Let's go get your stuff," I said, grabbing her by the hand. "I'm ready to get choo home."

"Where's home?"

"You'll see."

On the ride to the house Monique filled me in on how her shop was doing, and how Brian was handling his 'The Man' status. "I turned one of those back rooms into a playroom. Its full of toys, and the wall TV. stays on the Cartoon Network."

"That was a smart move. My Baby got it upstairs," I said, caressing her left breast.

"Yeah, I figured I should make it tolerable for the kids, cause they get restless fast."

"Business must be booming."

"Oh it has picked up. All of Brian's lil hookers come in. His ass is down there acting like he's the Godfather. When he steps into the club he starts buying the bar and dropping C-notes to have the V.I.P. section cleared for him and his team."

"He'll calm down eventually."

"I hope so. Them dancers call him 'Brian Da Benjamin.' They be in da shop gossiping. One day I heard one girl tell 'er friend, 'Da Benjamin came in and dropped about 8 gees last night.' I hate that he be letting them girls trick him outta his money."

I just smiled and didn't respond. Women don't understand that dudes getting money have fun in the titty bars blowing doh. It's just recreation.

We arrived at the house and when we went inside Mo looked around with a big cheesy grin on her face. As she continued to tour the house I called Rome and let him know where I was and that any visits would have to be solo.

Mo was in the bedroom when I got off the phone. "This is our love nest." I told her, as I wrapped my arms around her and kissed her on the neck.

"I love it, and I love you," she said.

She turned around and began to give me soft sweet kisses. Her breath smelled of cherries, which increased my desire to kiss her passionately. She stepped away from me and began to slowly undress as she stared at me. I wasn't as patient in removing my clothes when she seductively laid across the mink comforter on our king size bed.

Slowly removing her left bra strap I kissed her shoulder and neck as I undid her bra. Her titties were beautiful! The right nipple became hard as soon as my tongue lightly grazed it. While kneading her left breast I planted soft kisses on her stomach and side in route to her love tunnel. She took her g-string off and I gave the muffin my undivided attention. Monique was going crazy! After sucking on the lips, I gave the clit a lot of direct stimulation and by the time I started making love to her with my tongue, she was shaking.

"Are you ready fa this?" I asked, as I stroked my shaft.

Licking her lips she nodded her head yes. Her back arched when I entered her in the missionary position. After a few long slow strokes I put my arm under the small of her back and brought the pussy to me, as I really got to banging it. Just when I was ready to flip her over, so I could look at that big ole pretty ass, and beat it up from behind, I felt a tingling sensation flow thru me and continued to bang away until I collapsed on top of her.

Laying on top of Mo I looked down at her and said, "That was good! And its gon' get better wit' each room that we christen."

"Well get cha strength up nigga! I'm ready."

"Not now Love. C'mon, let's take a shower. I gotta show you off, and let choo see the city that teaches niggas how ta ball."

****

When we pulled up in front of Chuck's Millionaire Club I could tell that Monique was impressed by all the young sharp dressed individuals driving Benz', Beamers, and Jags. Inside the club men and women alike were draped in the finest linen that long money could buy. And the jewels were shining. A lot of eyes were on us. Monique was nodding her head to the beat as she led me to the bar.

"You trying to tell me somethin'?" I asked.

"Naw. I just wanted to sit down."

"Send me a fifth of Courvoisier over to my table," I told the bartender. "C'mon Baby. We ain't sittin' at no bar."

A few MCN affiliates were there, but not any of my actual crew members. However, if anything jumped off it could be handled. The waitress brought over the Yak, along with a complimentary bottle of Dom. Mo sipped on the Dom, and I tossed shots of Yak.

The dance floor was packed. All kind of eyes were on Mo as she was shaking her ass in front me. The liquor had me hyped and horny. I was rubbing her on her thighs and caressing her titties as I danced behind her. She was just as hot! Her hands massaged my erect tool while she brushed up against me and nibbled on my bottom lip.

Back at the table I pulled her down on my lap and whispered in her ear, "Girl you be working this muthaphucka," and gave her a pat on the rump.

I was biting on her neck when I heard someone say, "You sure keep you a dime piece on your arm."

When I looked up I was disgusted. Alex was standing in front of us with three other cats. His admiringly, yet disrespectful eyes shifted from Monique to me. I calmly picked up my drink and threw it in his face, and never taking my eyes off of his, sat the glass back on the table. Before I knew it his mans had 4-5's pointed at us.

Assuming he had the drop on me, his lips twisted up into a sardonic grin. However, the smug smirk that Alex had quickly became a look of panic at the sound of MCN soldiers cocking automatics as well.

Like a true drunk, it was too late before it dawned on me that I was slipping. BAD! My burner was in the truck, but I had no fear. "You scared ta push da button," I arrogantly asked, with a grim look on my face, "I ain't. We can set dis' bitch all da way off," I continued, my demeanor and the look in my eyes displaying my realness.

I felt every muscle in Monique's body relax when Alex said, "Don't do 'im now."

My mans were present, so there was no doubt that he would've died as well. And to be truthful, I wasn't phucked up about dying. I was more so phucked up cause I thought this lame was going to be the one to have me done.

Once the commotion died down I sent Twirk to get my truck and park out front so I could leave.

During the ride home Mo was very quiet. She just rode in silence. I could still feel a slight tremble when I reached over and grabbed her hand. "Baby I'm sorry I damn near got choo killed tonight."

I felt her turn to look at me. She gave my hand a squeeze and said, "Tay I was scared as hell! But I'd rather died with you than to go on living without you. I don't tell you I love you because it sounds good. I tell you I love you because I do."

I let a minute pass then looked over at her and told her, "I love you too."

I've been known that I did, but the moment was right for me to finally tell her. However, I was thinking about Alex more than I was thinking about anything else. I knew he was a soft ass bitch, and that night proved it. Had the roles been reversed he'd be dead. Hell, if I'd had my burner on me that night he'd be dead.

Chapter Thirty

Rome was sitting on the couch with Lil Rome in his lap watching the Pistons destroy the Kings, when Landa walked into the den.

"What's up Baby?" He asked, looking at her in the doorway. "You look good as hell. I like when you get your hair done like that. The look alone makes me horny."

Landa had just left the salon and had gotten a fresh do. She didn't get anything fancy done to her hair, she knew that Rome loved when she got those two braids laying over both shoulders, but instead of getting the ponytails braided, she left them silky strait.

"Where's Tay been?" She asked, sitting down next to him on the couch. "I ain't seen 'im in a while."

"I don't know. He's been busy. Shits been hectic since Sig's been in a coma."

"The girls in the Shop was talking about how they been seeing him out all hugged up wit' some dark skinned woman."

"I bet the girls didn't happen to mention how they always trying to give me some pussy," he said, never taking his eyes off the television.

"No! But I think its phucked up that he's playing Tasha like that. He could've at least took the bitch out of town."

"Baby them hoes probably lying. I ain't the only one they wanna get in bed wit'. And even if it is true, it ain't none of our business."

Looking at Rome with a whatever look, she said, "Oh you know it's true. And it is my business when it's my girl that's being played."

Lil Rome had fallen asleep, so he didn't yell. But he angrily looked at Landa and said, "Yeah that's yo girl! The same one that allowed us to sip drinks, sent by the nigga she was fucking! The same one that dude wanna kill my brother about. I don't wanna hear shit else about it. And you bet not open yo mouth." Landa sat back with a frown on her face and crossed her arms. She looked like a scolded child who had just been punished. "You hear me?" Rome asked her.

"Yeah, I hear you," she answered, in a low voice.

Rome felt bad that he had to get hostile with Landa, but the truth was the truth. Tasha's antics had been the cause of the war with the GN cats and they were pretty sure that Alex was behind the hit on Tone and Sig. He didn't want other people's problems to cause friction between them, but he also couldn't allow her to cause trouble between Tay and Tasha.

"You mad now, huh?"

"Nope."

"Yes you are. C'mere," he said, putting his arm around her, and pulling her closer to him.

When the game was over Landa took Lil Rome with her to the kitchen to start on dinner. Rome went upstairs and threw on some clothes so he could shoot up to All-Stars to meet Junior.

He walked in the kitchen to kiss his babies bye, and Landa looked at him like he was crazy. "Ain't you gonna put that up?" She asked, pointing at the .357 Desert Eagle he palmed in his right hand.

"Nope. It needs to be in hand at all times. The seconds that it takes to whip it could be costly."

There wasn't a lot of people in the bar when Rome walked in. Junior was at a back booth sitting down talking to a couple of dancers. Rome ordered some hot wings and a Heineken, then went to join Junior.

When he walked up, the dancer, Popsicle, moved over and said, "Have a seat stranger. I ain't seen you around these parts lately."

"The family likes me to be at home. And actually I can't be here long. I gotta holla at my mans then I'm out."

"I get the message," she said, as she and the other girl got up to leave.

He gave her a pat on the ass and told her, "I'll be out to play this weekend, so be ready." She gave him a wink and walked off.

"What's up Playboy," Rome said, giving Junior a play.

"Ducking da plain clothes, counting my green doh and fucking a few hoes all while I lay low."

"Been working on ya rhyme skills I see. I been holed up in da house playing daddy when I ain't at da spital sittin' wit' Sig."

"I ain't heard shit on da streets 'bout who was behind that. Niggas' keeping real quiet."

"That's because that nigga Alex is running a tight ship. Last week him and Tay had a run-in at Chuck's. Dude had Tay and his girl staring at several barrels, but told his mans not ta shoot."

"Strait up!"

"Hell yeah. Tay threw a drink in his face, so his mans drew down on 'im."

"I wonder why they ain't kill 'im."

"I don't know, but Tay was wondering the same thang. It's strange cause we basically know he put the hits on Tone and Sig. And Sig found out the he wants Tay killed. Tay don't be out much, so they don't run into each other. And we ain't got no leads as to where he lays his head."

"This shit is crazy as hell. But I'm ready to roll when it jumps off."

"I already know," Rome said, and signaled for the waitress to bring him another Heineken. "Oh, tomorrow we can get together so you can get right. I been laying so low and planning this wedding that I ain't even got shit in order yet. All my out of town people been hittin' me so they can hit da road. So shit will be in order tomorrow."

"That'll work. I been out about a week, but being out is the only way a muthaphucka can chill. But I'm always ready to get on. When we leave here we can shoot by my spot and pick up that change."

"Aiight. I really ain't..."

Junior started kicking Rome's foot. When Rome looked at 'im he started motioning his head toward the bar. Rome couldn't believe his eyes when he looked up and saw E. He had been outta sight for so long that Rome thought he had left town. Now he sees him posted up at the bar kicking it with one of the dancers like he's a Don or something.

E turned to look around the club and when he saw Rome there was no indication in his body language, or facial expression that he even wondered if Rome knew. Guess he didn't know that Rome had somebody like Pep on his team, that cut the grass so the snakes would show.

"I thought you was gon' get back at me," Rome said, when E approached the table.

"Dog, I got rid of that shit and jacked the change off. I ain't wanna hit choo without no loot, again. I'm on da grind now. You know a nigga don't stay down."

"Nigga that lil shit whatn't shit," Rome told E. "I already know it's hard to hold on to change when you're accustomed to gettin' paper. I got that shit all day, and was actually looking forward to mashing some on you."

"What if I hit choo later on tonight, or in the morning, can we hook up?"

Rome shook his head no. "Naw. I'm taking my woman outta town for a couple of weeks. We'll have ta get together when I get back."

With a frustrated look on his face, E said, "Damn!"

"Shid, if you got time we can roll out now. I gotta go tighten up my man Dee," Rome said, leaning his head towards Junior.

"Bet. Let me go tell this lil bitch that I'll get at 'er later."

As soon as E walked away, Rome looked at Junior and smiled. "Get a ride and meet me at your spot in 'bout 20 minutes."

****

Rome and E pulled into Junior's gambling spot parking lot. Rome made a call and Junior emerged a couple of minutes later through the back door with a green duffle bag. He stood by the black 745 BMW that was parked in the lot.

"C'mon. That muthaphucka got a cold stash spot," Rome told E, as he pulled out his burner and placed it under his seat. "And leave your burner."

"I ain't even got one on me."

Rome looked over at him like he was crazy. "You trippin'," he said, shaking his head as he got out the car.

"Ain't no way in hell I'm lettin' you drive. Give me dem keys," Rome told Junior.

Junior handed Rome the keys and stood by the back driver's side door. Rome hit the key alarm and the doors unlocked. Him and E got in the front and Junior climbed in the back seat. As they started riding

Junior said, "Damn its roomy back here," as he stretched out and laid his left leg across the seat.

They stopped at a red light on Meyers and Curtis. E was bouncing to Scarface' 'On My Block' when Rome muted the sounds and said, "The Center."

In the rearview mirror he saw Junior nod his head okay. Rome felt E's questioning glance, but didn't acknowledge him and turned Face back up. The light turned green and as soon as Rome started turning left on Curtis Junior shot E three times in the back of the head.

"Damn! You got that shit all over me," Rome said, making a quick right into the parking lot of the Northwest Activity Center, and wiping blood and brain matter off the side of his face with his hand. "Why you ain't shoot from my side?" He asked.

"My fault," Junior said grinning. "Just hurry up and park," he continued, as he began to squirt lighter fluid on the floor and all over E's body.

Rome parked in the back of the parking lot in the same corner where they used to strip cars after they stole them when he was young. Junior lit the back of E's shirt and he went up in flames. When they got out he set the back seat on fire and continued to squirt the lighter fluid until the whole inside was blazing. Rome took off his Al Wassam leather and wiped his face, then threw it into the fire. They walked into the center thru the back entrance and exited thru the front, and left in the black Chrysler 300 that was waiting.

****

Walking into the study, followed by two Federal agents, Landa had a nervous expression on her face. The last time the police showed up at their door Rome was hauled off to jail with a murder charge, and this time it was the Feds. Landa's stomach was in knots. She so desperately wanted Rome to get out of the game. And now she worried that his adversaries had come to remove him from the game, and her life.

"What's up?" He asked, as he set his Playstation controller down. "Who are you?"

The two white agents looked at each other. Then the one with short hair pulled out his I.D. and said, "I'm agent Landry and this is my partner agent Barney. We'd like to talk to you if you don't mind." Rome's facial expression must have displayed his dismay because Landry quickly added, "We decided to stop by rather than inconvenience you by bringing you to the Federal building." Rome remained silent, but motioned for them to have a seat.

"Do you know Eric Fleming?" Agent Barney asked him.

"That's E. Yeah I know 'im. Why?"

"He was a government informant. And he was found burned beyond recognition last week. We have reason to believe that you wouldn't want him around."

Rome kinda smirked before he told the agents, "Yall ain't got reason to believe no shit like that. We was aiight. We ain't have no problems."

The agents looked at each other, then Barney asked Rome, "Where were you last week?"

"Last week when?"

Agent Landry looked at his pad then said, "Last Tuesday at…"

"Da time don't matter," Rome said, cutting him off. "I was here all day. I ain't leave the house."

"How can you be sure?"

"Cause my woman gets her hair done, and I had my son. We stayed in, and when my woman got home we had a slight exchange about her wanting to tell her friend that her man was cheating. Then we spent the rest of the evening making up."

"Will she corroborate that?" Agent Landry asked.

Rome looked at the agent and yelled, "LANDA!"

Shortly after, Landa appeared in the study doorway. Rome looked at her and said, "They wanna ask you some questions," then continued to play his game.

Landa looked at the agents and Barney asked her, "Could you tell us where you were last Tuesday?"

She looked at Rome, but he was engrossed in his game. Then she turned her attention back to the agents. "I was either here or at the hair salon."

"Where you home alone?"

"Uh-uh," she said, shaking her head. "I was here with my fiancé, and our son."

The remaining questions that they asked only got them answers that coincided with what Rome told them. Frustration was all over both agents faces as they continued to probe. Their experience with criminals led them to believe that Rome knew what was going on with the case being built against him. They also knew, from experience, that without anything concrete, men like Rome wouldn't hang themselves.

Closing his note pad, agent Landry looked at Rome and said, "You are aware that murdering a federal informant is a serious offense."

"I'm aware that murder PERIOD! Is a serious offense. And I ain't do it. I ain't have no problems wit' 'im. I told yall that, and I'm thru talking. I'd appreciate it if yall would carry your warrantless asses up out my house," Rome said, eyeing both agents and standing up ready to lead them to the door.

Chapter Thirty-One

Me and Rome were leaving the hospital from seeing Sig when he told me about his visit from the Feds. We hadn't seen each other in a few days, so this was the first time I'd heard about it. It made me extremely nervous to say the least.

"So why did they come see you? Did they have a warrant?" I asked.

"Naw. They ain't have no warrant. They came to ask me some questions about Eric's murder."

"Who is Eric?"

"E. Dude who put them people on me. They found his burned up body in a car behind the Center," Rome said, with a smile on his face.

At first I thought that it was silly that Rome found the man's death amusing. Then it hit me! He was the one that did it. That's why they found the body behind the Center. We had left so many bodies back there that I was surprised that a camera hadn't been installed in that lot yet.

I glanced over at Rome and asked him, "When you knock 'im off?"

He went on to explain how him and Junior had lucked up and saw him at All-Stars, and how they were able to get him to leave with them. I was quite impressed with Rome's ability to put a murder plot together at the spur of the moment. Usually one might just wait until they got outside and shoot. But Rome showed patience and didn't allow his anger to overtake his thinking. I was kinda surprised that he didn't just have someone do it. However it was abundantly clear that he didn't hesitate to eliminate those that could bring him down.

While he was telling me all the details of the hit, I was thinking about the one that I wanted to put down. Me and Sig were supposed to have had him taking care of by now, but my dog was hanging on by a thread.

Pulling into the driveway at my house I looked over at Rome and asked him, "How Landa know what ta say?"

"I been told 'er that if we're ever questioned, if I don't stop 'er then answer the questions. But if we're solo, or I say I ain't talking without my lawyer, ta keep 'er mouth shut."

"Damn. I like that. I gotta put Tash up on that one." Rome just smiled. "You up for anotha one? Me and Sig were suppose ta holla at Alex, but now it's just me and you."

"You know I'm wit' choo. I figured that you was gon' have Carlos' hit team take care of that."

"I was, but I already made plans ta do it myself. Then that shit happened ta Sig and Tone, and I was gon' give da hit ta Los. But afta he called his self taunting me at Chuck's, and I made it up outta there alive, I made up my mind that I was gon' kill 'im myself."

"Kill who?" Tasha asked, as we were walking in the house. Me and Rome looked at each other then looked at Tash, who was standing at the door with her hand on her hip. She must've heard me pull up and was there to greet me.

"Tash I've told you before not ta question me about my business," I told her, as I walked in the house.

"I think I have a right to know what's going on, especially when you're planning to do something that could take you away from us."

"Baby I ain't going nowhere. And whateva I do its best that you don't know. I'm very cautious wit' every move that I make. The one time that I got knocked wasn't even my fault," I finished, cutting my eye over at Rome.

"Hey, don't dwell on da past," he said, hunching his shoulders.

Tash looked at him then back at me before she retorted, "I know you're talking about Alex. Tay, have somebody else do it. Baby I don't want choo to do things that you don't have too." She was staring at me pleading with watery eyes.

I saw the fear in her and began to feel sorry for her. Not only because she was so worried, but because of her naivety as well. Women seemed to think that money, or going to jail are the only parts of **Da Game**. They just can't understand the intricacies of it. And nothing backed that fact more than the fact that Tash was standing before me full of fear because I had to make a decision that she didn't understand.

"C'mere," I told her, wrapping my arms around her waist. Don't worry. I'll put it in somebody else's hands." I hated to lie to her, but as her man it was my job to put her at ease.

Relief was written across her face and she had a little bounce in her step as she walked out of the library.

"So when you wanna take care of that?" Rome asked.

"Probably when I get back from Ecuador."

"Ecuador?"

"Yeah. I gotta go over there and straighten out some shit. I been putting it off for the longest. It's almost time for your wedding, and I wanna take care of this so I can get back."

"When you leaving?"

"I don't know, but I'm a call my man and set it up a-sap. I won't be gone long, but it's a very important meeting."

****

Yahmo was catching a lot of flack from our Associates because I had been, what they considered, disregarding the importance of the meeting. So when I called him and told him to set it up he was relieved. I didn't know what to expect from the people that I was going to meet, but I was looking forward to it. This was the meeting that was gonna put me in a position to put the Midwest market in a choke hold.

Yahmo said that after we got the legal issues out the way that the business discussions would blow my mind. He said that in all the years he's been dealing with them they've never wanted to meet one of his Associates before. His words made me smile, and I was smiling now as I sipped on my second drink while watching the movie 'Swordfish' play on the airplane movie screen.

The flight to Ecuador was long and tiring. The sun was beaming and seemed to drain what little energy I had as I stood in front of the airport waiting on my ride. About 10 minutes passed before a medium sized man with a dark tan and thick mustache finally approached me. His accent was so heavy that I could hardly understand him when he asked me my name. After introducing himself, Alou grabbed my bag and I followed him to the red jeep that he was standing by.

The last hour and a half of the three hour ride was spent on dirt roads with little to no traffic. If someone did drive pass us, Alou knew them.

The ride came to a halt in front of a black 8 ft. security gate. Next to the intercom was a monitor, in which someone's face appeared, to see who was there to enter the premises. Alou waved his hand and the gate opened so that we could pass thru. It wasn't until we were about a quarter of a mile up the hill that a beautiful estate began to come into view. As the entrance road leveled out I saw the front of the biggest home I'd ever been too, personally. It was a striking example of design excellence and timeless style.

Nestled within this guard-gated private land, overlooking the Pacific Ocean was an extraordinary 18,000 square foot villa. An array of luxury cars decorated the spacious driveway. The two German shepherds that were resting at the front door didn't move, even after we'd exited the jeep.

Inside we were greeted by a man of Alou's stature that told me to follow him, as Alou took my bag and headed up the stairs. On the terrace, sitting down talking, was Yahmo and three other men. Yahmo stood and we shook hands. He introduced me to the gentlemen that were sitting with him. The first being a tall white man with glasses and salt and pepper hair. He looked like he was in his middle 50's.

I was trying to figure out where I'd seen his face when Yahmo said, "Tay, Senator Legion. Senator this is one of our dearest Associates." We shook hands then I turned my attention to the other gentleman that was standing as Yahmo introduced us. "And this is Javier."

"It is a pleasure to finally meet you," he said, with a heavy accent, though not as heavy as Alou's.

He motioned for me to have a seat. Me and the other gentleman acknowledged each other with a nod. We weren't formally introduced, so I figured him to be the loyal hit man, cause he did give off a dangerous vibe.

"Terrance tells us that you were not satisfied with the deal that was offered," Javier said.

"That is not completely true," I began. "We were willing to accept the deal that was told to me. It's the last minute change that we were not in agreement with."

"That was unintentional, but it does happen from time to time." The Senator told me. "All deals we propose aren't final," he continued, "but they're usually what we say they're going to be. Please understand that sometimes we have to compromise with our people, and that's when the changes come about."

I understandingly nodded my head, but needed them to understand me. Before I spoke I glanced at the quiet Little Man. His eyes were fixated on me, and he didn't blink one time. I looked back at the Senator and spoke matter of factly.

"I realize that changes occur. I also know that prison is a part of the game that we play in life. But that was my little brother that was gon' be compromised, and I wasn't willing to hand him over to the Feds for the next decade and a half. Plus, I raised him to deal with adversity, so I know that he'll stand strong and stare the enemies in the face when they come."

"It's always good to have faith in those that we are close too." Javier said. "However, it's unreasonable to think that everyone should trust him as you do. Everybody has people that they'll put their life in their hands, but we don't share that trust, and that's why we expect everybody to take the deals that we offer. But I'm only speaking about future instances now, because that problem no longer exist does it?"

I felt everyone's gaze shift toward me. It was unclear if they felt that the move could cause bigger problems, so I chose my words carefully. The last thing I wanted was for them to feel like I could be a possible liability and sick the little dangerous man on me.

"Luckily it doesn't," I answered. "My people were given strict orders to leave him alone. If he had too, my brother was prepared to change his identity and relocate.

"Thanks to you all," I said, gesturing with my hand to the men at the table, "our financial status would have allowed us to easily make that transition. However, the rodent was out partying and was spotted by reliable exterminators, who felt it was a once in a lifetime chance. Permission was sought, and granted. Now I assume that the investigation on my brother is bleak."

"That definitely steamrolled their case," said the Senator. "But will he avoid charges for the murder?" He asked.

"Most definitely. They questioned him and his alibi checked out."

"Wonderful!" Javier said, clapping his hands together. "How 'bout we eat, no?"

****

Dinner was delicious! We ate a dish that I had never heard of and couldn't pronounce the name of. During the meal the Senator did most of the talking. He threw quite a few names of some Judges that I should have my lawyer talk too. They were all on the state level. He explained that all Federal issues would be handled by him. He also gave me the names of some union heads that were gonna get my construction company some elite contracts.

He and Javier both shared a passion for dog fighting. We talked about various breeds and different matches that we'd been too. He was into cock fighting as well, and told me that he'd call me the next time any of his were fighting.

I was truly enjoying myself, but one thing was still on my mind. I was waiting for the right time to broach the subject of getting more work when the little dangerous man spoke for the first time. "I would like to speak with Mr. Manning alone," he said, as he stood up.

He was very small in stature. About 5'4" and 140 pounds with long shoulder length hair, a thick mustache, and a dark tan. Across his forehead was an old knife wound that was about 2 inches long.

I looked at Yahmo as the Little Man began to walk away from the table. Yahmo winked at me and nodded his head for me to follow the Little Man. I caught up to him and we continued to walk in silence. We passed two guest houses and a horse stable as we headed around the back of the grounds. Tennis courts and a Polo field also came into view as we walked toward some steps in the back of the house. The steps led to a dock with two boat lifts, and a primary dock with a 115 foot yacht. Once we boarded the yacht and reached the second deck the Little Man picked up a phone, in what looked like a lounge. When he hung up he headed behind the bar, and as he started to pour drinks I felt the yacht begin to move. The Little Man came from behind the bar and handed me a snifter with Brandy in it.

"Thank you," I said, as I watched him take a seat in the leather chair across from me. He nodded his head and took a sip of his drink.

Speaking in an even tone he said, "Mr. Manning I am very successful in our field because I am ambitious, and a very good judge of character. You managed to make a big impression on Javier, from afar. He always speaks highly of you. But I only trust my instincts. And before I make any decisions pertaining to any individual I must meet them. And I choose not to meet many people. But it sounded as if you were the perfect candidate."

"Perfect candidate for what?" I asked.

He put his hand up to stop me from talking, and continued, "The point of this meeting was for me to meet you in person. And by the way, my name is Felio."

"It's nice to know the name of the man responsible for my fortune."

His lips twisted into what I guess was his best effort of a smile. "There were three things that stood out during your conversation with our friends. First and foremost, you are a very intelligent man and your loyalty to your organization is to be commended. Your ambition is unparallel to any of our other Associates."

"That is true Mr. Felio. I am very ambitious. My mind is constantly working overtime on ways to expand all my business ventures, legal or illegal. I'm into expanding, and it appears that I've made contact with the man that can help me."

"Oh, I am that man. And how can we help you anymore than we already have?" He asked.

"Mr. Felio. I have a strong hold on the Michigan market, but that's not enough. I'm dabbling in Ohio, but I don't have the product to corner that market. It's ripe for the pickin'. I'm the man that can provide the leg work to control it and you're the man that can provide the most important piece. I would like to have a separate shipment from the one that arrives in Michigan, to go to Ohio."

"And would you like to have the same amount sent to both places?"

"Actually I would. I'd like for you to send as much as you want too. There is no limit on what I'd take. I think I've proven that I'm not only reliable, but trustworthy as well. What I get, gets moved."

The smile on his face was one of a man that liked what he was hearing. And he had to notice the sincerity in my words, cause I spoke the real and from my heart. He went and got the decanter and refilled our snifters. I assumed that he was mulling over what we had been discussing. But I soon found out that he was ready to move along. "Will your street affairs affect your business?"

His question caught me off guard. I was sure that he was referring to the war with the GN's. It was no need to downplay it, since it was obvious that he was fully informed about it. "No. It won't be a problem because I eliminate my problems. My opponent did an excellent job of masking his involvement, but the grass has been cut, and I will handle it as soon as I get back home."

"Mr. Manning I must ask that you bring no harm to Alex." My facial expression surely displayed my surprise at him knowing about Alex. "Yes I know him. And not that I have too, but I will explain the connection.

"You see, Alex is a major asset to us. He controls markets as well. Only he deals in heroine. He opened steel companies in various cities for shipping purposes. That is why he is not to be bothered. We will not tolerate anyone disrupting one who provides that kind of production."

His last statement upset me. And I'm sure that my anger wasn't lost in my tone. "So I'm not to protect myself? Or deal wit' an individual that is looking for my demise?"

Even when my dismay was shown he never changed his tone when he spoke. "Mr. Manning did you not understand what I said? No one who provides production will be harmed. You too are untouchable, so to speak. But you actually have an advantage."

"How?"

"Alex is weak for women, and that is why he was never a candidate for the position that you are now in. He also does not know who you are affiliated with. All he knows is that you are to be left alone. And I expect our relationship to remain anonymous. There are three men in the States that I am personally linked too. One resides on the West Coast, one on the East and now you from the Midwest. Before you leave you and Javier will finalize a new agreement, and that's who you will deal with on a business level."

I reached my hand out and we shook hands. I had just moved into a position that only two other people were in. Money was no longer my motivation for cornering markets. I was now on a quest for power. And with that trip I had acquired some.

"Thanks a lot," I said. "I really appreciate the trust and confidence that you have in me."

"No. Thank you Mr. Manning. Having you aboard is truly an asset," he said. Then his look turned serious, as did his tone, when he continued to speak. "Just remember that deals are non-negotiable, and Alex Bryant is to never be harmed."

Chapter Thirty-two

"Next month you'll be Mrs. Jerome Harris. We da shit! Our relationship has been full of bliss. I don't think I can be any happier," Rome told Landa.

They laid in bed engaging in pillow talk after an intense, hardcore sexual episode. "You know I cum so much harder when you're real rough wit' me, and flip and toss me around. And asphyxiation really heightens the orgasm, so you know how happy I am," Landa said, snuggling into Rome's chest.

Rome busted out laughing. He leaned back and looked at her with a look of disbelief. "Baby you're sick," he said, still laughing. "So from now on you want me to get Ike Turnerish when we fuck!"

"Naw," she said, with a look of embarrassment. "I love when you're sensual and you take your time making love to me. Us women like that because it shows that our mate is well rounded, but ain't nothing like wild uninhibited sex."

"Whew! Anything else I can do for you?" Landa's look turned serious, and Rome knew that the conversation was about to take a 360 degree turn. He was tempted to steer the conversation back to a less tense topic, but figured that they may as well get whatever is weighing on her mind out in the open.

"Well, I know that look. What's on your mind Baby?"

"Rome we're getting married next month, and I want us to grow old together."

"We will," Rome said, trying to assure her.

"Not if you continue to do what you're doing. It's time to focus on the legal side of things. Our kids, kids, kids are financially set. Why are you still in the Game? It ain't shit that we can't have."

"Landa we've been through this before. Some people go to Chrysler everyday, some people are teachers. Baby I'm a gangsta, and not in the sense of the word that these kids use it. You're right, it ain't about the money no mo'. We run an organization, and just because it's not F-E-D approved doesn't mean I'm going to stop," Rome said, as he got up and headed toward the bathroom. He stopped in the doorway and turned to look at Landa. "Besides, we're damn near untouchable. The state doesn't have the pull to stop us, and the government is as crooked as any of the activities that I'm involved in."

****

Rome and Tay were at the tailor getting their suits tailored for the wedding. They had been hanging out all day doing nothing in particular and decided to go to their tailor, Dom Caracani, and start getting their wedding attire together.

"Sig has been gaining his weight back, and since the incarceration is in two weeks I think he can get fitted for his suit," Tay said. "He ain't gon' put on that much weight in two weeks."

"What choo mean incarceration?" Rome asked in mock dismay.

Smiling, Tay said, "That's what marriage is. But maybe you're into confinement." Rome gave him a light elbow in the side and laughed. "Naw, I'm just phuckin' wit' choo. This move is gon' complete choo. You're successful, yall already got a seed together, so this is all that's left ta do."

"What about choo? When you gon' tie da knot?"

Tay looked over at Rome and said, "I don't know. I'm still trying to get past that Alex shit. She hurt me wit' that one dog."

His answer brought about a deafening silence. They remained quiet for the rest of the time that they were in the shop. On their way over to Sig's house they mostly talked about the upcoming match between Tay's 38 pound Red Boy female against some dudes out of Texas' dog. As always, Tay felt that it would not only be a win, but a kill.

"You know Linsey 'bout ta get anotha kill under 'er belt."

"How many she got?"

"One. But what made it special was that it was against a 4 time winner, and it was her third win."

"Well a win is good enough for me. I'm a take all bets fa whateva. Them dudes think they da only ones getting money. We gon' kill they dog and hurt they pockets. You think Sig gon' go?"

"I doubt it. He's only been out the spital for a few weeks. He ain't even got all his strength back yet."

When they arrived at Sig's house Tay cut the car off and sat back. "Dog I ain't think dude was gon' pull thru. And I surely didn't think I'd be coming over here again," he said, as they got out of the car.

Keisha answered the door. She sat wit' Sig every single day that he was in that coma. Sig had a lot of visitors. Rome and Tay were at the hospital often enough to be on a first name basis with most of the staff involved with Sig. But Keisha didn't miss a day the whole four months that he was in his coma. True to her word, she was right by his side when he woke up.

"What up doe Ms. Ride or Die?" Tay said to Keisha, when she opened the door.

"Yall. Ya boy in the kitchen eating. Would yall like something to eat?" She asked, as we headed toward the kitchen.

We told Keisha that we were alright. She headed in a different direction and we went into the kitchen. Sig was putting his dishes in the sink, and nodding his head to the music when we walked in. His keen senses must have kicked in because he turned around with a look of suspicion.

"Man I must be paranoid as hell," he said, when he saw that it was us. "I felt somebody staring at me, but I knew that it wasn't Keisha."

"Its only us," Rome said. "We just left Dom's, and was on our way home when you called Tay and said to come thru. What's up?"

"Remember I told yall that my memory was phucked up?" Rome and Tay nodded their heads. "I been putting shit together in my mind and I figured out what happened." They looked at him with questioning stares. "First let me ask yall this. Who all came to see me in da spital, that should have?"

Tay sat back in his chair and thought for a second before he spoke. "Uh, Blue off da Eastside. Lou, Bino and everybody from your crew. Even some of the lil soldiers. Hell, Ito even flew up a couple of times to check on you."

"Okay, let me ask you this," Sig said. "Who didn't come up to da spital?" Rome and Tay were looking bewildered. "Man yall slow! Que! I bet Que didn't come see me."

"Naw. I ain't neva see 'im when I was up there. And we were both up there quite often," Rome said, looking at Tay, who shook his head "no," as well. Rome looked back at Sig and asked him, "So you think Que was involved in the hit?"

"I know he was. He was there at the spot."

"What! What spot?" Tay asked in high pitched voice.

"Just listen," Sig told him, with smirk on his face. "The day I got shot he called me. He was like, I got these cats that's throwing a party, but they need some hoes. I knew what he was talking 'bout, so I was like, why you ain't call ya mans, talking 'bout you," he said, pointing to Tay. "And he was like I called 'im but he ain't answering his phone. Since I knew you was out of town I asked 'im how many. He was like, 50. When I said alright, he said tell 'im ta be at the club at five.

"Right before I got ready to leave, Tone and Trina came thru, so I told Tone to ride wit' me to drop the work off."

Tay put his hand on his forehead and said, "Damn, he just happened to be there. Tone wasn't 'spose ta get killed and shouldn't have gotten shot. I phucked up."

"How?"

"I forgot to tell you that I cut him off, but after I talked to Que I called Ace and told 'im to finish Que off. That's probably why I didn't call you right away."

Sig had a satanic grin on his face and started nodding his head. "Well its really coming together now," he said. "Ace is the one that killed Tone and tried to do me.

"When we walked in the Soft Dick Club, Que, Ace and about three other cats were at the bar chillin'. I figured the unnamed dudes was the ones that wanted the work. Shid, at the sight of Que and Ace, me and Tone was in chill mode, but they ain't hold us up. While Que was pouring drinks, Ace drew down and put da thang ta Tone's head. I ain't have my burner on me, but I knew them niggas was 'bout ta kill us. Tone did too, cause he made a move and that's when Ace buss'd 'im. I just reacted. I jumped off da stool, wit' da intentions of rushin'

Ace, but he put the barrel on me wit' da quickness. Next thing I know I'm waking up in da spital sore than a muthaphucka."

"I wonder why they didn't do clean up, and finish the job," Rome thought out loud.

"The actual act of killing them two probably phucked Que up, and he was ready ta roll. I bet Ace hit choo in the chest first," Tay said, looking at Sig. "He figured you was finished wit' da face shot and they disposed of yall in da alley behind da club where yall was found."

"Yep," Sig said, nodding his head. "But I wonder why Ace flipped on us?" He asked.

"I don't know. But I do know that we're gon' find out. They probably done left town, but I know how to get 'em ta come home," Tay said. "Afta Rome's wedding we'll deal wit' them clowns."

****

The sun was out, and the light breeze gave the day the perfect touch that an outside wedding needed. Over 200 guest had come to attend the union of Rome and Landa. Double that amount were expected to be at the State Theater for the lavish reception. Tay had pulled strings so that Belle Isle was theirs until 6:00 p.m.

Rome stood at the altar in his tan suit awaiting his bride to be. In carmel colored suits Tay and Sig were at his side, looking dapper as well. But all eyes were on Landa as she was being escorted down the aisle by her Uncle George. Rome felt like he was the luckiest man in the world as he watched her stroll toward him in her white Vera Wang wedding dress. Tasha and Trina both had tears in their eyes as they viewed their girl prepare to be the first of them to fulfill every young girl's childhood dream.

Rome looked over at Landa as she took her place beside him and said, "Baby you look beautiful!" She smiled and they turned to face the minister together.

Chapter Thirty-Three

"In da house is his mother, grandmother and sister. She's in high school, so make sure she's home before yall run up in there. I want all of 'em," I told Chris. "Once that's accomplished, and their secure at the Eastside spot, hit me."

After Rome's wedding I took Tash and Tay to Disney World and Six Flags in Georgia. Upon our return I got 'The City' operations on track, then headed down to Ohio to finally get shit moving down there. A lot of dudes from different parts of Ohio traveled to Detroit and other states to get work cheaper than it was there. And thanks to me they could now stay in-state.

I stayed down there for a few weeks, but came back early because Tash was approaching her due date, and MCN had some personal matters to resolve.

"I can't wait ta see this hoe ass nigga Que," Sig said, when Chris left the bar.

"It won't be long," I said. "As soon as he finds out that we got them he'll pop up." Sig just nodded his head with a pleasant smile on his face. "When is Rome coming back?" I asked. "I ain't seen his ass since they left for their honeymoon."

"Man, that fool is so in love it's scary. They came back from Hawaii while you were in Ohio, stayed home for 'bout three days, now they're in Tahiti."

"What! You bullshitin'?"

"Nope." Sig answered, laughing and shaking his head. "He said they'll be back in a couple of weeks."

"Man he trippin'. We got shit to do. I hope he's ready to leave the nest next month. Once Tash drops our load we gotta get on da grind again. I'm goin' back to Ohio, and one of yall gotta network in Indianapolis and the other one in Louisville. The line is wide open! You ain't gon' find nobody that can beat our prices."

Full of enthusiasm, Sig said, "You know I'm wit' dat! I'll take Naptown. I used ta phuck 'round down there, so I got a inside track on politickin'."

"Mo's brother is a hustling fool. Brian got niggas coming to Dayton from Columbus, Cleveland and Cincinnati ta get thangs. I'm just going back down there to smooth out da daily operations. He has a keen business sense, but I think I can make 'im a more polished player."

****

"We got 'em."

"Aiight. I'll be there in 'bout 20 minutes."

When the call came thru, Tash and I were going over a list of some sites that we were looking to buy. She wanted to start bringing her visions to life. Her first being a strip mall. And location is everything for a real estate developer.

As soon as I hung up the phone I called Sig. When he answered I told 'im, "My man, meet me at da house on Fisher and Gratiot." I told Tash that I had some important business to take care of and I'd be back as soon as I finish, then I left.

When I pulled up in front of the house I saw Sig's Monte Carlo parked across the street. He answered the door with a .40 cal in his right hand. "Wait til you see who we got in the basement," he said, as I walked in the house.

First we walked into the kitchen where Que's mother, sister, and grandmother were in chairs with handcuffs on their wrist, and duct tape over their mouths and ankles. They were wearing blindfolds as well, which was good, cause I didn't wanna have to harm them. I noticed specks of blood on Sig's shirt, but said nothing. We left them in the kitchen with one of Chris' mans watching them, and headed downstairs.

Chris and anotha one of his mans were sitting on an old washer and dryer smoking a blunt. In the middle of the floor sitting in a chair was a bloody Ace with his hands cuffed, around the pole, behind his back.

"Well I'll be damn," I said. "Where yall find this lame at?"

Chris started grinning then said, "You ain't gon' believe this. He hit me yesterday right after I left your spot." He looked at Ace and his expression turned serious. "It was so coincidental that I was kinda leery. Then he told me that he needed some work, so I told 'im ta meet me in da Kettering parking lot. When he got there we scooped 'im up and brought him here ta get on," he said, laughing.

"The ladies were down here," Sig started, "but I had them transferred upstairs. That way they won't hear me slapping him up, and not wanna call dude."

I was thankful that Sig's anger hadn't clouded his ability to think. Cause if they play hardball we would've had no choice but to play harder ball. And like I said before, I didn't want to hurt them.

"Dig Chris, go upstairs and tell da momma, or da sistah that we'll let 'em go for $100,000. Get one of them ta call Que and let 'em talk long enough to say 'they got,' then bring da phone here, wit' him on the line."

Chris headed upstairs and I headed toward Ace. He stared back and forth at me and Sig with a look of pain on his face. The gashes in his head were bleeding profusely. He looked like he was hurting, but he didn't look scared. I guess he knew what the end was gonna be, and that fear couldn't save him, so he may as well die with his pride.

"What made you flip on us Ace?"

"He ain't said shit since I been here," Sig answered. "Even been takin' his dome shots like a man."

"Ace, I always knew you was a strong dude and whatn't no rat," I said, looking at him. With a look of pity on my face I continued, "But you're a snake! And they die too." As if on cue, Sig cracked him across the right side of his face with the burner.

When Chris came back downstairs he handed me the phone. As soon as I put it to my ear, I said, "Que we need ta talk."

In a paranoid voice, he asked, "Tay what's up? Why you doing this?"

"Que. We need talk."

With tears in his voice, he said, "Tay I ain't did shit!"

"I'm gon' say this one mo' time. Que! We need ta talk."

"Okay. I'll be home tomorrow."

"Good. Now listen. They don't know who has them. That's because I plan ta let them be. But if you're not at your mothers by 8:00p.m. tomorrow, one of 'em goes, and I'll start the clock over. But the same rules apply."

I closed the phone and tossed it to Chris. Sig smacked Ace in the face with the burner again, then turned to me and asked, "What's next on the agenda?"

I looked at Chris and told him, "I want you to have somebody posted up on Greenview to pick Que up when he gets there. If he ain't there by the set time, have them call you, and do the sister. Then call 'im and let 'im talk to one of the remaining two, so he knows that we're serious. And call me when he's here, or all three women are gone."

"Consider it done," Chris said, nodding his head.

"And we can head home," I told Sig.

He nodded his head alright, then smacked Ace in the head with the burner again. Then we left.

****

The call came thru about a quarter to six. I called Sig and told him to meet me at the spot. We both arrived at the house around the same time. I was glad that this shit was coming to a head, and I could focus on business again.

In the basement the scene mirrored the one from the previous night, the difference being, Que was cuffed to another pole. Sig wasted no time drawing his .40 cal and smacking him across the face with it. Intensely watching, Chris and his mans sat quietly smoking a blunt.

I leaned against the wall and asked Que, "How much did you tell the Feds?"

"I ain't tell da Feds shit!" He responded, in an angry tone. "They was investigating me, but they ain't have shit. You trippin'."

"So what made you flip on us?"

He just stared at me.

"Answer 'im," Sig growled, then cracked him in the head. His head snapped to the side, then he slowly raised his head and stared at Sig, then me. "Answer 'im," Sig said, and raised the gun again.

Que flinched and stuttered, "O-okay. When I found out da Feds was on me, I figured you was gon' cut me off, or have me hit, so I started laying low. Afta we talked at Dibo's I thought we were strait. Then Ace confirmed my first suspicions when he told me that you gave him da order."

Ace looked over at Que in disgust. Que paid no attention and continued, "But I whatn't gon' snitch."

"So why you try ta do Sig, and kill Tone?" I asked.

"Chips told me ta hit Sig and Rome, but ta leave you alone."

Sig gave me a look filled with confusion, but I understood what was happening. He couldn't touch me, so he wanted to wipe out my mans. Que started phucking with dude when I cut him loose. Again, Alex had allowed his plans to fall into my lap without being executed.

"So you switched teams on me." I stated.

"Tay it wasn't personal," he said, in a pleading voice.

I pulled out my .45, with the silencer on it and told him, "Neither is this." I shot him twice in the face.

I trained the gun on Ace, but before I pulled the trigger I heard Sig say, "You bet not." With a smirk on my face I looked at him then passed him the mag. He put three in Ace's mug, then looked at me and said, "Yeah. That was personal."

I told Chris to clean up and cut the hostages loose, then we left. It took us about 30 minutes to get to Dibo's. We grabbed a fifth of Louie and went into my office. Sig twisted up a blunt and we proceeded to get right.

I explained to Sig how I wanted to do things and how we had entered into a world that didn't exist to millions. He didn't like the fact that we couldn't kill Alex. I couldn't tell him why, but he assured me that even though he doesn't know why, that he'll trust my reasoning. The fact that we had political contacts had him ecstatic. And the contacts were wherever we were. Mr. Felio made sure his people, in The States, were connected with whomever could keep them free to handle business.

****

September 23, 2004 Tash gave birth to our little girl, Dontaya. Tash already had everything, so I couldn't think of anything to get her for having the baby. Then I thought of the one thing she wanted, but didn't have. I left the hospital and didn't return until the following morning.

When I walked in the room she was breast feeding Taya, and gave me a grim look. "I'm sorry Baby," I told her. "I know you're upset, but I had to go do something really important."

"I see it was so important that you forgot to go pick up Tay from mama and daddy's house."

"You leave today, so we can scoop him up on the way home." I told her, as I sat on the bed. Then pulling out the ring box I said, "But I want choo to leave as my fiancée." When I flipped the box open her mouth dropped open at the sight of the 7 carat ring.

"Will you do me the honor of being my partner for life?"

With tears streaming down her face, she responded, "You know I will."

****

We spent a lot of time together from that day forward. Mainly because I knew I had to go down to Ohio, and didn't know when I'd return. Plus it was nice being daddy to my infant. I'd missed out on all of that shit with Tay, so I was enjoying it then. The Holidays were truly enjoyable, but after New Years it was time for me to get to work.

Chapter Thirty-Four

I stayed down in Ohio for about three months. That allowed me enough time to be with Monique, and get Brian some connections in places other than the streets. I only had 150 chickens a month coming thru Elijah Slaughters for the time being. Brian could handle that, and if he needed more in a few months I'd have Javier increase the shipments.

Sig had established a means to have work shipped strait to Indianapolis. Louisville was still untouched. Rome said it wasn't going anywhere, and he'd get to it eventually. Me and Sig were loyal to our marriage, 'The Game,' but Rome's loyalties laid with Landa and Lil Rome. And I couldn't be mad that his priorities were intact.

****

We were on our way to All-Stars for the first time in a long time. I glanced over at him as he twisted a blunt and said, "It's nice to get some time out of you. We finally gon' have a playas night out, and you wanna hit All-Stars."

"Ahh! My brudder miss me," he said, pinching my cheek. I smacked his hand away and laugh. "Dog, I just be chillin'," he started, "cause Landa wants me to leave the game alone. So I figure if when I'm not taking care of business, and I'm wit' her, she'll stop nagging me about it. And as far as hittin' All-Stars, since we're out, I wanna flirt wit' Popsicle."

"Oh you wanna knock 'er off, huh?"

"I said flirt. I'm doing that faithful thang dog. On da real, Landa completes me, and I'm happy as hell."

For it to had been a Thursday, the bar was off the hook. It seemed like it was full of the upper echelon hustlers. Grants and Benjamins were all that were being passed and tossed at the women dropping it like it was hot. The waitresses were getting their flirt on, and collecting money as well.

We caught some playas' leaving a back booth and copped a squat. Before we could order any drinks the waitress arrived with a fifth of Armadale. "From the man at the table," she said, pointing toward a booth in the corner.

When we looked, my man Keith threw his hands up and mouthed, "What up doe." I hadn't seen Keith in years. He used to cop from me before I went to the joint. And from the sparkling I seen around his neck and wrist, it looked as if he was doing well. But I knew I could beat his best prices, so I planned to holla at him before we left.

Females immediately made their way over to our booth. "Look, here comes the sluts fa bucks," Rome said, as four girls we hadn't seen before approached.

They were about their business too. They knew what it took to make a man hit their hip…kissing, dancing, spanking each other. The show they were putting on for me and Rome was the beginning of a freak show. On the stage two girls were in the 69 position giving each other's love box attention. Every dame in the joint unleashed their bi-side, and got paid.

However, Rome didn't see the whole show. He crept off to the back with Popsicle and didn't return until it was almost time to leave. When he came back and sat down I just smiled and shook my head. "Dog, she got the best head on this side of the Mason-Dixon line," he said.

"You a silly man. C'mon, let's roll."

Outside in the parking lot I peeped Keith standing beside a black Yukon Denali talking to one of the bouncers. When I walked up the bouncer gave us both a play and left. I noticed that he had something soft in the passenger seat, so I decided to be brief. "Dig dog," I began, "I just wanted to let choo know that choo should get at me on whateva."

"You back on wit' da bomb?" He asked.

"Nigga da work better and da prices sweeter."

"Quit playing! If you on like dat I got mucho business fa you. Give me a number, and I'm a hit choo tomorrow," he said, pulling out his phone.

I began to rattle off a few contact numbers when I sensed some tension. My first instinct was to spot Rome, and when I did he was by the entrance fighting. It was like deja'vu. I quickly headed toward the altercation, but before I got there, a scene that would change the rest of my life unfolded before my eyes.

Even though I was running, everything seemed to happen in slow motion. I started yelling Rome's name when I saw one of the spectators whip his gun and shoot Rome two times in the back of the head. His body went limp and he hit the ground, face first. The gunman began to back peddle toward the alley eyeing me with an evil smirk on his face.

I was oblivious to all the running and screaming that was going on around me. Falling to my knees I grabbed his limp body and rolled him over. His eyes were closed, and if not for the gash on his face, from the fall, he'd look like he was peacefully sleeping. I embraced him, holding his head to my chest and began to cry.

I don't know how long I stayed like that, but the next thing I knew an officer was touching my shoulder saying, "come on son." When I stood up I noticed that no one was in the parking lot except police and paramedics.

The officer that touched me was an older man in his 50's. He said, "I know you may not be up to it, but I need to ask you a few questions."

Looking at him, I said, "I don't know what happened. And I didn't see shit. All I know is that my brother is gone, and I gotta go tell his wife that her husband is dead."

He asked me my name, wrote it down, and nodded his head. As I was walking toward my car I heard someone calling my name. I looked toward the crowd, standing behind the yellow tape I saw Popsicle waving me over.

When I walked over to her, she said, "I took it off 'im" she began, as she placed Rome's wedding ring in my hand, "while you had 'im."

I looked into her swollen, puffy eyes and said, "Thank you." Then I asked her, "You need a ride?" She shook her head "no," and I left.

When I pulled up in front of Rome's house it was 4:47 a.m., and I couldn't believe that my visit wasn't to see him. I sat in the driveway for about 20 minutes. I was unable to get the image of his bloody face out of my head. It was hard for me to think strait. I wanted someone else's family to feel the pain that I was now feeling, but I had no idea whose it would be.

On the surface it appeared that he was shot by a friend of the dude he was fighting. But the look on the killers face said that it was more to it than that.

The clock on the dash read 5:22 when I finally gathered my senses and got out of my car. The walk to the door was long and dreadful. I rang the doorbell a few times and waited. After a couple of minutes I heard Landa say, "You bet notta lost your keys." Then I felt her look thru the peep hole. She opened the door and backed up as I walked into the house. At the sight of all the blood on the front of my shirt, and the grave look on my face, the tears started rolling down her face, and she asked, "Tay, where's my husband?"

Tears began to find their way down my cheeks as well, and I was too choked up to speak. I just walked toward her with my arms open. We embraced and stood in the foyer crying.

****

The rain and sunless sky made the day of the funeral even more bleak. Landa and Lil Rome had been staying with us, but I was hardly home. I found it hard to be around anybody. Sig had comeback as soon as he was notified. But I'd only seen him once over those last six days. This was the hardest thing I'd had to deal with since Elijah was killed.

My thoughts were interrupted by a knock on the study door. "Yeah," I said, in a voice that was barely audible.

"Baby the limos' are here. And Sig just pulled up."

"Okay. Here I come."

Me and Sig rode in one limo. Tash, Landa, my Aunt Tina and the kids were in the other one. I needed to prepare for the task at hand. Landa and Aunt Tina were gonna need for me to be strong, and I couldn't gather the strength, being with them then. Discussing the actual events of that night, and thinking about a payback allotted me some solace.

The church was full. There were quite a few dancers there, and Rome had tricked with them all. His second love was tricking with strippers, mine was Monique—who was also at the funeral. She told me that she was gonna come to pay her respects when I called and told her what happened.

Once they closed the casket Landa passed out and missed the funeral. Trina and Tash took her home. The burial left me angry and hurt. Aunt Tina remained strong throughout the whole thing, and I was amazed at the strength that black women could muster up when most people would fall apart.

Back at the house we were actually enjoying ourselves. I had everybody laughing as I talked about some of the silly shit that Rome used to do, and it was a lot of silly stuff. The reminiscing must have been getting to my Aunt Tina, cause she took one of the sedatives that Tash had given Landa and went upstairs to lay down.

Trina went to answer the door when the doorbell rang. She came back and said, "Tay, its some kinda delivery for you."

I went and signed for the long white box, with a black ribbon on it. Unsure of what it was, I went into my study to open it. Inside was a dozen of black roses, and an envelope. I pulled the card out and five thousand dollar poker chips fell out. The card read: Hope you're enjoying this day as much as I am!

****

The last stunt that Alex pulled sealed his fate. Thinking and planning a way to get him never crossed my mind. The following morning I went to Bryant Steel. Just like I figured, his arrogance would work in my favor. His office was on a floor with no one else's.

When I got off the elevator his secretary was at her desk.

"Can I help you?" She asked.

"Is Alex in?"

"Whom should I tell him is here?"

"Oh don't worry 'bout it." I gave her two chest shots with the silenced tool.

He was sitting at his desk working when I walked in. At the sight of me with the burner in my hand, his eyes got real big. "I ain't into games," I told him, walking directly at him. The first shot caught him in the shoulder and he flipped over in the chair. I quickly rounded the desk, leaned down and dumped five in his face. Blood shot up in my face. I wiped that shit with my arm, turned and left.

****

I went over Sig's when I left Bryant's. After I got outta the shower we sat down and kicked it while we blazed a blunt. "Dog, puttin' 'um in his ass was better than a nut. Now that this hoe ass nigga is dead we can focus on business. No more unnecessary beefin'."

"Yeah, that's cool, but I wish you woulda done that different."

"Man I'm strait. It was eight in da mornin'. The majority of the employee's work outside, or in a different building from the offices. And the location of his office was da icing on da cake."

"Nigga, as mad as you are, you woulda killed his ass in front of the Senate."

I chuckled and said, "You probably right."

Chapter Thirty-Five

Almost three months had passed since Rome's murder, and I was still learning how to cope with him being gone. In so many ways losing Rome hurt worse than Elijah's death. I had been playing the crib a lot. If it wasn't business then I wasn't interested in doing shit. Chilling with my family made me happy.

Me and Tash were laying in the den watching **Training Day**, but I just couldn't get into it. I stopped the DVD, and asked Tash, "Baby, when you gon' set a date for our big day?"

"I'm ready now, but I wanna give Landa some time to heal. She's still an emotional wreck right now."

"I know. I truly feel her pain. You should tell 'er to move. She's either here or at her moms house, cause she doesn't wanna go home."

"Alright. I'll talk to her. But how 'bout we practice for the honeymoon while we have the house to ourselves."

For hours we made love throughout the entire house. At some points it was slow, soft and sensual. At other times it was intense, loud and hard grudge fucking. We started in the den, but by the time I bust'd my fifth nut, that produced no fluid, we were on the pool table in the basement staining the felt with sweat.

After that episode we took a shower, got dressed in our fine linens and went to a cabaret at Cobo Hall.

The party was on and popping when we got there. Unlike the cabarets I used to go to when I was 17 or 18, drinks were available, free of charge. That's to be expected being that it was given by Chris Webber. The champagne fountain was flowing, and every table kept a full decanter of Louie. The only people in attendance were people who'd try to find the owner of a Rolex if they found it.

Me and Tash knew quite a few of the couples that were there. It wasn't flooded with hustlers either. The ones that were there were well connected, and into major legal ventures as well. We mingled a bit, had a few drinks, then hit the dance floor. The DJ was spinning everything from Roger Troutman and Run-DMC to Jahiem and Jadakiss. We danced for hours. By 3:00 a.m. I was tipsy and horny.

I made my rounds saying goodbye to the few people that were still there then we left. When we got home Tash gave me a quick dose of good loving and we both fell into a deep coma like sleep.

The phone woke me up the following day at about 1:00 p.m. I looked over at Tash, but she didn't move. Liquor always did her in. When I answered the phone I was unsure of who was calling.

"Tay. What's up dog?"

"Shit. Who dis'?" I asked in a harsh tone.

"Brian nigga."

"Oh. What's happening my man?"

"That's what I wanna know. I been tryna get in touch wit' choo for 'bout a week."

"Man I been in a world of my own. What's up? Somethin' wrong?"

"I don't know. Last month my woman's period was late. And this month it didn't come at all. I done got nervous, that's why I called you ta see what's up."

I knew what he was talking about, and it was strange cause my shipment up here hadn't come either. "Let me get up and get myself together. I'll call you back," I told him. I needed to make some calls and see what was going on.

While I was in the shower Tash came in to use the bathroom and told me, "Baby, Sig just called and said he's up at Dibo's waiting on you."

"Aiight."

"And mama just called and said Tay can stay, but it's time for Taya ta come home, so I'm 'bout to go get her."

"Okay," I said laughing. "I'm a go holla at Sig, and I'll be back ta spend the day wit' my girls."

Tash opened the shower door, gave me kiss and said, "I love you baby," while she fondled me.

"Love you too girl."

****

When I walked in Dibo's, Sig was at the bar talking to Marcel. We went straight to my office, and as soon as I closed the door Sig started talking. "Did somethin' happen? I ain't got no work in two months. Last month I just figured it couldn't get there, cause you know that happens every now and then. But this month I knew somethin' must be up."

"Hold up. Let me see what's da deal," I said, reaching for the phone.

My first call was to Yahmo. When he answered the phone I asked him, "What's da deal dog? My system is having a few glitches. What can you tell me?"

"Call Jav dog," he said, and hung up.

I just looked at the phone and hung it up. Sig noticed the funny look on my face and asked me, "What's wrong?"

It was time for me to tell Sig what was going on, cause I didn't know how serious shit was about to get. Things were beginning to unravel, and I wanted my people on point. A war could be in our future, and we wouldn't be caught off guard. We may lose the plug, but we wouldn't lose the war.

"Dig," I began, "the contract I agreed to had two stipulations."

"What were they?" Sig asked.

"One was that deals they arrange would be taken. And the second one was to leave Alex alone."

"Where do he fit into this?"

"He was on da same line that we're on, except he was gettin' boy. I knew that, but he didn't. All he knew was that I was ta be left alone."

Sig dropped his head then looked back up at me. "And you broke da contract when you laid that fool down," he said.

"Yup," I said, nodding, "I did that. So I guess da plug is over."

"Ahh," Sig said, snapping his fingers. "Who'd you just call?"

"Yahmo."

Sig got a questioning look on his face and said, "Yahmo?"

"Yup. That's how it all started. He hit me off after I went ta see 'im, and we ain't looked back since."

"Well I'll be damn. So now da beef is on wit' dis fool and his mans."

I started shaking my head. "Naw. It's deeper than that."

Sig's face became a mask of consternation. "Huh!" He said.

"Dog, he turned me on to the head man. That's where da political contacts come from. And that's why I could get what I wanted when I wanted it."

"So what did Yahmo say to have you looking so crazy?"

"He told me to call Javier, and hung up."

"Who is Javier?" He asked, looking baffled.

I went on to explain to Sig how Javier was the man that me, Yahmo and some dude on the East Coast contacted about business. Then I told him about my trip to Ecuador and the meeting with the Little Man. When I told him how it was intended for our organization to control a whole region, the disappointment of the missed opportunity was etched on his face.

I sat back in my chair, threw my hands up and said, "And that's everythang."

He stared at me for about a full minute, rubbing his index finger across his top lip like he was in deep thought, before he spoke. "So you done crossed a muthaphucka named Felio!" He said. I couldn't do nothing but laugh. "We 'bout ta have lil bitty foreigners coming over here trying ta see us?"

"Possibly," I answered.

He clapped his hands then said, "Phuck it. Lets get ready ta set dis bitch off."

"I'm 'bout ta call Javier and see what he has ta say. "When I got Javier on the line I merely asked him, "Jav what's da problem?"

He responded by saying, "When you get over your anger call me and we'll resume business. Our motives are never personal." Then he hung up.

I relayed his response to Sig and we just looked at each other, unsure of how to take what he said. We kicked a few ideas back and forth between us, but overlooked the obvious. Expecting a light payback we decided to put everybody on point and prepare for war.

After we smoked a couple of blunts and threw a few shots back I headed home. During the ride home it hit me that me and Sig had an important discussion and Rome wasn't there. Damn, that shit hurt like hell. It wasn't until I pulled into the driveway and saw Tash's car that the sadness left me.

As I was opening the door I could hear Taya yelling. When I took a few steps into the house I saw Tara sprawled out on the floor bleeding from the neck. I immediately started yelling for Tash, and following the sound of Taya's cry.

The sight in my bedroom killed what piece of a soul I had left. I picked my baby up out of her swing, and kneeled down and put my other baby's head in my lap. I closed her eyelids and peered at the gunshot wound that pierced her heart.

As I held my weeping child and my lifeless better half, I felt empty. It never occurred to me that they were on some you kill my man I'll kill yo bitch, now we're even shit. I was smart enough to run a multi-million dollar drug enterprise, but not keen enough to put together the riddle that could've possibly saved my woman. I was heartless, and vicious enough to wipe out anyone who betrayed, or posed a threat to me. But I was not dangerous enough to prevent my Associates from killing my soul mate, and I gotta live with that for the rest of my life.

*KEEP WATCH FOR GROWN MAN PUBLISHING
NEXT PAGE TURNER…*

HAPPENSTANCE

BY Thell

The Main Character

Ace and Luke went back to grade school together, airtight from day one. Luke was a killer way back then, he just hadn't killed nobody yet. In school they started a crew called the *Aces,* that was their beginning.

Ace was the leader, and Luke was the muscle, now, 20 years later, it's still like that. Then came Donny, they hooked up with him in the 5th grade. Donny didn't do no talking. Donny didn't play no games. At recess, right after lunch, Donny demanded money from every kid on the playground, of course it was just small change, but Donny said it, that was it, so the *Aces* enforced it. That introduced the gang to extortion. Donny had a beast mentality that was unreal for a child his age. In just a short time, after Ace and Luke met Donny, the *Aces* became the Ace Organization, went from some school boy shit to a hood thang, and that's when them *boys* turned into them *guys.*

Ace didn't come up like Luke and Donny. Ace's Daddy, Big Ace, was a old playa. He was strictly business. *Get money.* Big Ace headed a mob that ran after hour spots, number houses and brothels, but the bulk of his money came from heroine, and O'boy, they had plenty of it! Big Ace was King of the City. Back when niggas rode Volvos and Audis, Big Ace drove a 500, triple white with windshield wipers on the head lights. Looking back on it, his Mercedes was sitting on 20" rims, and that was back in 1977! So fuck what you heard, if your money is right, you can get whatever you want. It doesn't matter whats out and whats not.

Big Ace kept a woman that looked like Lucy Liu, or Kimora Lee. He had a real thing for those types. It wasn't until Ace got older before he realized why his father dealt with so many Asian men and women. But everybody else knew. Especially the players, it was that China White heroine, shit, what the fuck! Big Ace kept the best dope in the city, way before Butch Jones and the Young Boys Incorporated back in 1978-79.

The Old Man was a old gangsta. His name went back to Max Julien, and the Mack. Lil'Ace use to laugh at pictures of his Daddy in $70,000. button up mink coats that drug the floor, matching big brim mink hats with feathers in them, tight silk shirts with fly away collars and plaid bell bottom pants. But seriously, Lil'Ace was the only person who laughed cuz Big Ace wasn't no muthafucking joke.

Rumor has it that the Old Man was tied in to the likes of Lucky Luciano and Meyer Lansky. It also holds that his ties further extended into Murder Incorporated, and the Purple Gang, as far as Detroit is concerned. But nobody can say for sure because the Old Man never said much. What we do know is that he shot dice, played poker and got drunk with gangsters like Mr. Wingate, Old Man Lindsy, Frank Nitty, and Milwaukee Jack, in all the gansta spots like *Pat's Lounge* on Gratiot, the *20 Grand, Chick Springer's,* and *Stokes'* on Chene.

X

Big Ace raised Lil' Ace around real deal ganstas, men that slid him balled up $100. bills and said, "stay in school, boy." Lil'Ace always wore the best that
money could buy. The boy had everything except what every boy needs, a mother, but Big Ace made up in game, all that his son would never get from the womb that birthed him. It hurt, but life hurts, and that's how the Old Man taught him to deal with it. "The longer you live, the more tolerant you become."

From the minute Lil'Ace was old enough to play little league football his father signed him up, he loved it, they both did, father and son. The Old Man never missed a game, or a practice for that matter. And every morning, regardless to what went down the night before, Big Ace was up early cooking breakfast and
getting his boy ready for school. One morning, while Lil'Ace and his Daddy sat at the kitchen table enjoying breakfast, 3 men laid hog tied and gagged in the basement waiting to be tortured and murdered for trying to rob one of the Old Man's number houses. Big Ace was a super dad, as well as cold-blooded killer.
Saturday morning, Lil'Ace's birthday, and not only that, it was big game day. Lil'Ace's little league football team went undefeated for the season. He was the starting QB for the American League Northwest Detroit Cougars, and today, they had to play the undefeated PAL League Westside Cubs in the little league version of the NFL Super Bowl. Both teams were highly talented and very well coached. The Cougars, blue and white vs. the Cubs, red and white. The Old man was more excited than his son, and as usual, he got out of bed early to cook breakfast. He polished Lil'Ace's football helmet so it would be nice and shiny for
the big game. He even had the cleaners to clean his son's uniform. Big Ace bought Lil'Ace a brand new pair of blue and white Nike cleats. He bought him
some blue wristbands with a white number 6 on them, he bought his son a pair of crispy white sanitary socks and another pair of blue wristbands to wear on his ankles. That made the Old Man smile, *wristbands on his ankles, boy o' boy, youngsters. O'well, that's what the boy wants.* Filled with pride, love and joy, anticipating how happy his son would be a few hours from then, the Old Man was lost in his own thoughts caught up in the moment when suddenly he felt a quick presence that shook him back to reality.
Before he could react, four masked men where immediately upon him in his kitchen. They were young men, he could tell by the looks in their eyes. They all had guns. The Old Man could sense that they were itching and panicked. They weren't professionals. That made the situation much more dangerous. Four kids, loose cannons, hungry. "Where it at old muthafucka?"

Enraged at the disrespect, Big Ace said, "Right here muthafucka!" At the same time, shots reigned from the pocket of his silk bathrobe where he kept a Colt .45 ACP. Straight gangsta mack to the end, Big Ace emptied the clip of his .45 while being riddled by the 9-millimeter bullets of the two masked robbers that he couldn't chop down.

Awaken by the blasts, Lil'Ace ran to his father and found him lying in a pool of blood. He fell to his knees and cradled his father's head in his arms and held him while he screamed uncontrollably facing the sky, as if to ask God why. Gasping to breath, choking on flem and blood, Big Ace shook and died. He would never get to see the big game, and he would never get to sing Happy Birthday to his son.

Send order form with check or money order to:

**Grown Man Publishing, LLC
P.O. Box 514
Jeffersonville, IN 47130
canonharper@icloud.com**

Shipping address:

NAME:_____

ADDRESS: _____

CITY:_____ STATE: ___ ZIP: _____

PHONE:_____

EMAIL:_____

TITLE	*QTY*	*SUB-TOTAL*	*TOTAL*
SUB-TOTAL	$
SHIPPING & HANDLING $6/BOOK $4 EA ADDITIONAL	$
TOTAL	$